Totally Bound Publishing books by Crissy Smith

Single Books
Seduced by the Neighbour
Lacey's Seduction
Eternal
Bid High
Fated Love
Vamps in the Ci

I0542055

Were Chronicles
Pack Alpha
Pack Enforcer
Pack Territory
Pack Rogue
Pack Community
Pack Mates
Pack Daughter
Pack Hunter
Pack Council
Pack Security
Pack Beta
Pack Secrets
Pack Balance
Pack Investigator
Pack Law

Corporate Wolves
The Favour
Losing Control

Secrets
The Shifter and the Dreamer

Shifter Chronicles
Birds of Prey
Bear Claw
Eye of the Tiger
Coyote's Kiss

Wolf Pack
Lion's Claim
Hidden Hyena

Bloodlines
Bite
Control
Embrace

Antholgies
Caught in the Middle: Magical Ménage

Collections
Bite Me!: Savage Love
Summer Seductions: Summers' Girl
Cloaks and Daggers: Vampire Hunter
What's her Secret?: Last Call
What's her Secret?: Designated Alpha

Bloodlines

FAMILY

CRISSY SMITH

Family
ISBN # 978-1-78686-393-5
©Copyright Crissy Smith 2019
Cover Art by Cherith Vaughan ©Copyright April 2019
Interior text design by Claire Siemaszkiewicz
Totally Bound Publishing

FAMILY

Dedication

For my family who loves and supports me every day.

Prologue

"Argent residence."

"I need to speak with the Elder Argent. This is Agent Smith from the Organization," he said calmly. He wondered if it was the same housekeeper from his childhood. Veronica had always been kind to him, but Kieran didn't recognize the voice on the other end of the phone line, so he didn't say anything else to her. Using his new name was a ploy to test how much his father knew about his new life.

"Please hold." He didn't know why he expected music. Instead Kieran just heard silence. Long minutes went by before he heard a familiar voice.

"This is Elder Argent."

Kieran had to close his eyes. His father's voice. He never thought he'd hear that sound again.

"Hello?" his father barked.

"It's Kieran," he said.

There was a moment of pause. "Son?"

"Yes." Kieran swallowed. "I'm calling you with some news."

"Go ahead."

There were no questions about how he'd been. His dad probably didn't care.

"Marcel and Elijah have been arrested and are in the custody of the Organization. They'll be processed in the morning, so you should expect a phone call."

"I take it they're in Las Vegas with you."

So his dad did know where he lived. "Yes." Kieran didn't know what else to say. A small part of him just wanted to hang up. He should have let Caspar call. But he was a man and he needed to face his fears.

His dad sighed. "I suspected as much. I'll give their father a call and let him know."

"You don't sound surprised," Kieran commented.

"As I said, I suspected that was where they went. My brother informed me they were out of town. I didn't ask questions. It's a logical assumption they'd go after you."

"Well, they failed."

"That's obvious, as it's you ringing me."

"And have been arrested."

"You already said that. There's no need to repeat yourself."

"You don't care?" Kieran asked. Was there no love in his family at all?

"If they were stupid enough to fail and get caught, then they must suffer the consequences. It's of no matter to me."

Fuck, Kieran came from this man. If his life hadn't been detoured at eighteen, he might be exactly like him. "Okay... Well... I just wanted you to hear the news about Marcel and Elijah from me. I guess I'll let you go."

"You don't have anything else to say or ask?" His father sounded disappointed.

Kieran huffed. "What do you want me to say, Dad?"

"How about asking after your mother or sisters?"

Guilt tore at him. "Why?" He channeled his anger. "Have they asked about me? Ever wondered what happened to me?"

His father's silence was enough of an answer.

"That's what I thought," Kieran said.

"What about asking to come home?"

"Why would I do that?" Kieran inquired. "You sent me away. Told me that I needed to become a man."

"And from the reports that I'm getting, you have. It's time for you to return to your family."

"Family?" Rage consumed him. "I have my family here. I don't need you."

"The humans and shifters?" His father scoffed. "You're an Argent. It's time for you to stop playing around and take on your responsibilities."

"I'm not playing around. I have a job that I'm good at. I'm in love. I have friends who'd do anything for me," Kieran told him. "I don't need you."

"You will. What's going to happen when your humans die of old age? Or when your lover falls for one of her own kind? I know all about the people you surround yourself with. The only one I approve of is Jackson Wickham. He'll be a good contact for the family."

"Listen carefully," Kieran demanded. "Stay away from my friends and me. Do not try to contact me. Just leave us alone."

"You don't understand, Kieran. This isn't a choice you can make. You will fulfill your destiny."

"My destiny?" he spat. "Are you fucking kidding me? I'm done with you. With the entire family. I'm sorry I even called."

"But you did. Because you have obligations to us. I'll give you two weeks to return. At that time, you'll take your place at my side."

"Not going to fucking happen," Kieran responded.

"And, Kieran, I disapprove of coarse language. That is something you'll have to curb. It's unbecoming."

"I don't give a shit," Kieran taunted, "what you approve of."

"Two weeks, Kieran. Or I'll retrieve you myself and you don't want that." His father hung up. He actually hung up on Kieran.

Kieran roared before throwing the phone across the room.

Chapter One

"Are there more pillows on the bed?" Dakota Reese called to her lover. Kieran Smith was in the bathroom, shaving before they headed into the office. "I swear the mountain of pillows keeps growing."

Kieran walked out of the adjoining bathroom, toweling off his face. "I have no idea what you're talking about."

She snorted. Her big bad Walker might have the rest of the world fooled, but she got to see another side of Kieran. A sweet and needy side that would shock others. One that enjoyed the softest of blankets and plush pillows. He hated to be cold, so the number of covers had also slowly increased over the last couple of weeks. "Sure, whatever you say, darling." Dakota eyed him as he stood in only a tight pair of boxer briefs.

Her arousal spiked like it always did when she looked at him. With the face of an angel, a body of a model and as dangerous as anything or anyone alive, being with Kieran still amazed her.

"Wasn't it you who complained about being late when I joined you in the shower this morning?" he asked, the teasing smirk just made him sexier. Of course he knew what she was thinking about. Hell, her pheromones filled the entire suite.

Dakota glanced at the clock next to the bed. *Damn, he's right.* If they were late another morning, she'd never hear the end of it from the other agents. It was hard enough keeping Kieran from torturing his co-workers—he did have an evil streak—but when they gave her or Kieran shit, it was worse. Kieran felt that if they could joke with him, then he wasn't working hard enough on being scary.

"You're thinking about it," he singsonged.

"Shut up," she mumbled. Dakota stomped to her closet on the other side of the room. She loved the elegant suite they lived in. They owned their residence and Kieran managed to take advantage of every aspect of living in a full-service hotel. Not that Dakota minded. Housekeeping came in daily and while they had a kitchenet in the suite, they ordered room service more often than not. The restaurants inside the hotel casino were five-star caliber and she could barely boil water.

Kieran's warm chuckle followed her as she grabbed the closest pair of black pants.

"Ah," he said, coming up behind her and wrapping his arms around her waist. "Don't be mad." When he nuzzled the back of her neck, she almost said fuck it and dragged him down to the closet floor. But they'd been on vacation for the last week and really did need to get to the office on time.

"Go get dressed," she ordered.

He grunted but released her.

Before he could make it too far out of the closet, she whirled around and slapped his ass. "But keep that thought for after our shift."

He grinned at her and Dakota felt all was good in her world again.

It hadn't been easy to convince him to get out of the city for a week. As much as Kieran claimed that he hated Las Vegas, he was comfortable there. But with the threat of his father coming after him, Kieran had been reluctant to go. She'd finally used the one tool she had to convince him—a week on the beach, with her in a bikini. The days away had been wonderful, but now it was time to return to real life.

She dressed quickly and within half an hour they were out of the door and in the parking garage. Her company SUV was next to his bike. Even though they were going to the same place, Dakota hated having to separate from him. They worked on different teams, so it wasn't as if she'd get to see him for the rest of the night.

Kieran pulled her into an embrace and she might have held on tighter than normal. Luckily, Kieran didn't comment on that. "Be careful. It's been two weeks and my father's actually crazy enough to show up."

Dakota cupped his face. She knew that she'd soon be meeting the elder of the Argent clan. No one doubted Kieran's father had been serious in demanding his return to the family. "If he's stupid enough to come here, then he'll learn real fast just who your family really is."

"I love you." He closed his eyes and took a deep breath. He was saying the words more, but Dakota didn't need them. She knew how Kieran felt. Had known even when he'd been fighting to accept her as a shifter as well as a lover.

Her jaguar tried to push to the surface, wanting to soothe him. The animal in her wanted to comfort their mate. Sure, they hadn't actually taken the final step of her claiming him, but both her human and shifter side agreed he was the one for them. It was only a matter of time before everyone else knew as well.

"You are mine," she said with a fierceness that surprised even herself. "He can't have you."

"Thank you," he whispered.

She gave him a quick kiss before pushing him back. "Now get to work. And stop trying to tempt me into following you back up the stairs."

His grin was wicked as his eyes sparked with mischief. "We haven't done it in a company vehicle yet."

Dakota laughed. "And we're not going to! I still can't look Caspar in the eye after what happened in his office."

"Oh yeah." His voice grew husky. "That was awesome."

This man, her lover, was a bad influence. "Work," she ordered.

"Yes, ma'am." He sent her a cheeky wink before stepping back next to his motorcycle. Well, shit, he'd taken her for a ride, sexual and non-sexual both, on that beast. She needed to get a little distance.

Dakota turned and opened the door to her vehicle. Behind her Kieran was turning the ignition on his bike. She resisted, barely, the urge to turn around and watch his ass as he bent over. *Work.* Work was what she needed to concentrate on.

He took off. Fast. No surprise there so she was left alone in her vehicle and to her own thoughts. For two weeks she'd been doing everything in her power to take Kieran's mind off his father. If the Elder Argent showed up in their town, he'd find nothing but trouble. What kind of father kicked out his own child in order to teach him to be a man? If that hadn't been bad enough, Kieran had been taken captive by a group of shifters and tortured and experimented on for ten years. Never once had Kieran's family searched for him. Dakota could have lost Kieran so many times before she'd even met him. Her life would be so different, boring, if not for Kieran.

Kieran's father was as much as a monster as those who'd caged Kieran to experiment on him. Dakota would not allow her lover to be hurt ever again. She strongly believed that Kieran's father had known about his extraordinary abilities and wanted them for himself. It wasn't until Kieran had started to make a name for himself in their underground security organization that there'd been any contact from the Argent clan. And that had been two cousins who'd tried to kill Kieran so they could be groomed as head of the family. *Like they're in the fucking Mafia or something.*

She shook off her thoughts then started the car. *Control.* She'd been working hard on remaining in complete control of her jaguar form. Dakota had her own issues that were going to have to be addressed, but her attention couldn't be given to anything other than keeping Kieran safe and with her.

The drive to the office didn't take long. Dakota kept an eye on the vehicles around her, making sure she wasn't being followed. Kieran's cousins had been on her tail a few days before she'd known about them and she wouldn't make that mistake again. She was a damn well-trained agent in one of the most secret and dangerous organizations in the world. Being followed by two morons was just embarrassing.

At the entrance to the underground parking structure, Charlie stepped out of the guard shack.

"Morning," he greeted. "Welcome back."

"Thanks." She smiled at him. "I take it Kieran's already here?"

Charlie shook his head. "I didn't even see him. I heard the door slam shut of the shack and turned, but no one was there."

She had to press her lips together so she didn't smile. *Kieran and his pranks.* He made it his mission to mess with the guards and other agents. Kieran claimed he was trying to make them into better agents, and Dakota had to agree he kept them on their toes. Charlie was the only one who embraced the challenge. The others made complaints to their boss, Caspar. "Did he lock you out again?"

"Ha! He tried." Charlie grinned. He dug in his pocket and pulled out his key ring. "I never set my keys down anymore."

"That's funny. Good for you."

"He texted me and said *good job* so he must have been watching."

She nodded. It wouldn't surprise her. Kieran didn't show affection like a normal person. The fact that he constantly screwed with Charlie meant that Kieran liked the young agent.

"Although I have no idea how he got my number," Charlie stated.

Dakota did laugh this time. "I don't ask questions anymore. Sometimes it's better not to know."

"Well. I'll be ready for his next scheme," Charlie said.

"That's a good idea," she responded. "Now that you passed his test, he'll up his game, so watch out."

"I got this," Charlie said with confidence.

"How's the field training going?" she asked. All young field agents started as a guard while they completed the extensive years-long process of advancing. It wasn't as though the agent could ever quit, since the Organization enrollment was about bloodlines and not voluntary, so the training was above anything else in the world.

"Great. I go to the range every morning to work on my marksmanship. I'm getting better."

"I'm sure you are," she said. "Keep at it and let me know if you need any help at all."

"Thanks, Dakota!" He tapped the top of her SUV before going back into the small building to open the gate.

Dakota drove through and parked in her usual spot. She didn't see Kieran's bike, but he preferred to park a couple of blocks away. Probably a good idea, as much as he screwed around with the agents who worked with them. Eventually someone was going to get Kieran back. Dakota dreaded that day. If Kieran had an actual worthy opponent, there was no telling how bad the pranks would get.

She locked up her vehicle before heading to the stairwell. She used to use the elevators, but since Kieran preferred the stairs and she figured she could get some extra steps in. She didn't spend much time behind the desk, but there were days when the piles of paperwork seemed to grow magically.

Just as she stepped onto the floor of her office, her phone chimed. She pulled it up to see the message reminder of the meeting about to start. Dakota dropped her bag on her desk before grabbing her tablet and making her way to the conference room.

Dakota was surprised to see Kieran there and in a seat. The half-dozen other agents were settled as far from him as they could be. Kieran didn't care one way or another about what people said or thought about him, but Dakota wanted to growl. If Kieran considered someone a friend, there wasn't anything he wouldn't do for them. The other agents needed to realize that.

Caspar was glaring at him, though, so he must have gotten himself in trouble in the few short minutes before she arrived.

"What'd he do?" she asked Remy, Kieran's partner, as she sat between him and Kieran in the spot she knew Kieran had reserved for her. As far as Kieran was concerned, that would be the safest place. Dakota was certain that nothing would happen inside the fully secured building, but it was just easier to go with Kieran's quirks.

"I'm not sure," Remy responded. "It has something to do with an email and hacking Caspar's computer."

"Shit." She should have been more suspicious when Kieran had called Mitch, an IT expert they'd worked with in the past. Mitch worked with Kieran's oldest friend and the Walker who owned the hotel-casino they lived in. Jackson only hired the best, so Mitch was the best, and Kieran using him didn't bode well for how their return would go.

Kieran chuckled. "It was soooo funny."

Caspar growled but didn't respond. As a human he probably hadn't heard the actual words, but he'd be able to see the smile on Kieran's face.

Dakota's partners, Gabe and Dare, were the last ones to enter the conference room. Dakota had spoken to both men the previous night and learned that they didn't have any open investigations. Hopefully Caspar had something for them this morning. Dakota didn't want to spend the day in the office.

"Now that everyone is here, let's get started," Caspar said. He moved to the front of the room, grabbing the remote to the monitors as he walked. "I received a report this morning that concerns me deeply. You should all have a summary on the share drive."

Dakota set her tablet on the table and powered it so she could follow along and make notes. Remy did the same while Kieran was kicked back in his chair with his hands behind his head. Kieran might seem like he wasn't paying attention, but he would be taking in every piece of information and mentally filing it away for later.

Still it pissed off the other agents, and that was Kieran's main goal.

Ducking her head to hide her amusement at her lover's antics, she gave her attention to the boss.

"Last week the Alpha of the local Pack contacted me about some strange incidents out in the Red Rock area. Signs of rituals," Caspar started. "He has his Pack patrolling the area, but this is an Organization matter. It needs to be handled quietly and quickly."

Dakota perked up more. She'd worked with the Alpha previously and found Damon to be a fair and kind shifter. He had a large Pack to oversee and they'd kept in touch. Even Kieran spoke with the Alpha off and on.

"Dakota, you're lead, with Dare and Gabe backing you up," Caspar said.

She nodded.

"Talk to Damon and go out to the site. I want a report by the end of your shift," he ordered.

"Will do," she replied.

"For the rest of you, make sure you're paying attention while on patrol. I have it on good authority that there's been an increase in shifters coming to town." Caspar raised his hands. "It might be nothing. If these are honest and well-behaved people who just want to enjoy their town, I want them to be able to. However, you know that the more shifter species together, the higher we run the risk of humans getting involved in incidents."

They all nodded. Since shifters had come out to the public, there had been numerous incidents of humans getting involved in shifter business. Getting hurt or hurting a shifter.

"We received calls about wild animals in the streets behind the Strip. It might just be dogs, but with the number of shifters in the area, we need to be sure. We're still fighting a battle with how humans perceive shifters, so we don't need more trouble." Caspar looked at Kieran.

"All patrol units need to keep an eye out. I suspect it's a few young shifters getting drunk and losing control of their animals. I want that stopped.

"Also, I want everyone to welcome our newest team. James and Caden will start their patrol tonight. Remy, you and Kieran have the closest assigned area to them, so keep an eye on our new guys."

Dakota glanced over at the newest agent duo. James, human, had transferred from Wyoming, while Caden, lion shifter, had recently completed his field training. She'd seen the email when catching up the previous night. Caden looked barely old enough to be in the field, although her jaguar shouldn't have a problem working with the lion shifter. Their species were close enough that they wouldn't have conflict.

Kieran sneered at the lion shifter, though, so she knocked his elbow with hers.

Kieran would need to be a mentor and there really wasn't a team better than Remy and Kieran for the job.

As a wolf shifter, Remy was part of Damon's Pack and could guide Caden in working with the Alpha. Kieran would make sure James had no weaknesses because he was human. The human agents were trained right along with the others.

"Finally," Caspar said, "I want every team looking out for any Walkers that they don't know. There is a possible threat directed at us and our agents. We need to have all our bases covered. We all know how rare and dangerous Walkers can be," Caspar didn't look at Kieran that time, although Dakota was certain it was Kieran's father who was the threat. Caspar wouldn't put the spotlight on Kieran, though, unless he had no other choice, which Dakota appreciated and she knew Kieran would as well. "We're lucky that we have our own Walker on our side. If you spot any unusual guests, get hold of me or Kieran.

"Keep your eyes open even when not patrolling. With winter here, tourism will increase now that it's not above one hundred degrees. I want the people here safe and free to enjoy their visit to the city and spend their money in the casinos."

A murmur of agreement went around the room.

"Any questions?" Caspar paused for several moments. "Then get to work."

Usually Kieran was the first out of the room, but now he hung back. Dakota gave him one last look before following Dare and Gabe out of the room. As much as she wanted to linger and check on her lover, she needed to get back in the field. Kieran could take care of himself. She just wished she could be there with him.

"How was your trip?" Dare asked.

"Great." She smiled at him. "But I think Kieran was antsy to get back."

"I bet," Gabe said. "I'm surprised you got him to go at all."

She shook her head. "He needed it." Regardless of the power that Kieran held, he was still that hurt and scared kid who had been through hell. Not many saw that side, but Dakota knew Kieran like no one else. Sure, he put on a good act, but if someone looked close enough, they'd see how much Kieran craved connecting to others. He was also hiding how much it hurt that, even after all this time, his father only wanted him for his power. The Elder Argent had tossed his son aside at eighteen with no concern for his welfare, but there was a part of Kieran who remained tied to the man and the family that had abandoned him.

It took every ounce of her control to follow along with her partners and ignore the need to go check on Kieran one last time.

"So where should we go first?" Dare questioned.

The investigation, that was what she should be thinking about. "I'll give Damon a call and see if he has time to meet with us," she said. Dakota was already pulling her phone out of her pocket.

"I need to grab my bag from my locker," Gabe told them. "I was running late this morning and didn't get a chance."

"Meet down in the parking garage in ten?" she asked. "If I can't get a hold of Damon we can go to the sites he told Caspar about. I have the file with the locations."

"Sounds good," Dare agreed. Gabe nodded.

They separated in front of her office and she went inside. Dakota merely needed to grab her bag, but it would be quieter to call Damon from there as well. She sat behind her desk but left the door open in case anyone else needed to speak with her before she went out.

She scrolled through her contacts until she reached the Alpha's name.

"Dakota," he said when he answered. "You and Kieran are back?"

"We are," she said. "And already back to work."

He hummed. "Then I'm hoping you're calling to tell me that Caspar put you on our case. This is very upsetting for my Pack and me."

"I am," she responded. "And to ask if you'd have the time to meet with me and my team. I want to get this solved as soon as possible."

"I agree. I'll make time to meet you," Damon said.

"Great. I'll read the file on the drive but what can you tell me?"

"Well," Damon drawled, "we've found three different spots that it looks like something weird is happening at. All within my territory and in open hiking areas. I don't like it."

"What do the sites look like?"

"There's a circle drawn on the ground with blood. Animal blood. Some of the rocks have been defaced with symbols that appear to be satanic. I'm pretty sure they're sacrificing small animals—natural animals— but still."

"I understand," she said. One of the reasons that shifters had decided to band together and announce their presence was because of the hunting that was killing human shifters.

"I doubled patrols, but the area is so massive that we can't be everywhere at once," Damon stated. "This last one was two nights ago, so we suspect tomorrow night they'll return. I'll have every available Pack member out."

"I'll make sure we have people as well," Dakota assured him. "I haven't shifted out there in a while." Not since they'd killed the shifters who'd been responsible for Kieran's capture and torture.

"I appreciate any help we can get. As matter of fact, why don't I meet you at the first location we found and we can look at it together?"

"Sure," Dakota agreed. "Give us about an hour."

"See you then." Damon hung up and Dakota noticed Kieran leaning against the doorjamb to her office.

"You're meeting the Alpha?" he asked.

Dakota nodded slowly. Kieran was better about the Alpha, but he still didn't like shifters, so it was hard for him to accept him. "He's going to show us the sites."

"Okay." He pushed off the frame and stalked across her office until he was leaning over her. "Be careful. It's probably just some humans being idiots, but you never know."

"Damon thinks they're sacrificing animals," she told him. "I want to catch these bastards."

"You will," he said with confidence.

"Did Caspar say anything about your father?"

Kieran shook his head. "He sent Angel and her boy-toy down to keep an eye on the family estate, but they reported everything seems normal."

"You know she'll kick your ass if she hears you call her mate that," Dakota teased him. Angel, Kieran's ex-partner, was another Walker who had mated with a wolf shifter in the panhandle of Texas and transferred closer to her mate. That had left Kieran and Remy to move to the Vegas office where Dakota had run into him.

"She can try," he quipped.

Dakota just shook her head before kissing him. She kept the contact brief. They were in the office, after all. "I've got to go. I'll see you at home."

"Home," he repeated. "Yeah."

Dakota enjoyed this softer side of her lover and wished that everyone else got to see him like she did. "You be careful too."

"Always." He stuck his hands in his pockets then rocked back on his heels. "Love you." He strode away, not giving her a chance to respond.

She stared after him watching the flex of his ass under his tight jeans. Jeez, now she couldn't wait to get home.

* * * *

Kieran stepped out of the office building into the cool night air. He liked being on the night shift when the action around town was heavier. Not that he had a problem being in the sun, but it was a lot easier to blend into the shadows at night.

"Ready?" Remy was leaning against one of the SUVs, twirling the keys in his hand.

"Yep." Kieran climbed into the passenger side, knowing Remy wouldn't let him drive anyway. One time—*one time*—he'd jumped out from behind the wheel to chase a suspect and Remy hadn't forgiven him. Remy had been fine after the vehicle Kieran had been driving crashed into a tree.

Remy walked around the hood of the SUV then settled behind the steering wheel and turned to Kieran. "No word on your father?"

"Caspar says he's still in Texas," Kieran said carefully. It wasn't that he didn't trust what information his boss had—Kieran just knew his father better than anyone else. If his father wanted to slip out of the Argent compound, he would. As good as Angel was, she didn't know how the Elder Argent thought. There was a good chance that his father suspected Kieran would have someone watching the family house. Kieran's father hadn't gained so much power by playing by the rules.

"You don't think so?" Remy asked.

Of course his partner knew his moods and could read him better than anyone. Well, except Dakota, who had the uncanny ability to know him better than he knew himself. "I think that we know what my father wants us to know."

"What do you want to do about it?" Remy asked.

That was the question Kieran currently struggled with. Part of him wanted to ignore the possible threat, stick his head in the sand and pretend nothing would go wrong. But the more mature part of him knew that if he didn't prepare himself, his father would be able to surprise him. Kieran didn't care what his father said or did to him, but the Elder Argent wouldn't go directly for Kieran. He'd try to hurt those close to him. So, Dakota, Remy and Caspar would be the most likely targets. Jackson was most likely safe, since his father had already mentioned using Jackson as a connection for the family.

Jackson, his friend from his days in captivity and owner of the hotel Kieran and Dakota lived in, was filthy rich and ran the Walker community of Las Vegas. He had the loyalty of other men just like him. Kieran's father wouldn't risk going after him for that reason alone. Add in the fact that, as a Walker himself, Jackson wouldn't be as easy to take down. No, it was the humans and shifters he'd grown fond of who would be in real danger.

"Kieran?" Remy asked. "You okay?"

"Yeah." Kieran shook himself, literally, so he could focus. "I'll talk to Jackson and see what his people have found out before I decide anything. I just think this is going to be above what the Organization can handle."

"We have the highest trained agents in the world. Our network is extensive and we have our own Walkers on staff," Remy argued. "Plus, Jackson and his people are civilians."

Kieran shook his head even before Remy finished speaking. "You underestimate Jackson."

Remy snorted. Kieran wasn't surprised by his partner's response. Remy wasn't fond of Jackson even though they'd worked together several times in the past. Remy was a firm believer in what the Organization stood for. He trusted the company that they both worked under.

Kieran wasn't like the other agents. He'd had a choice. After Caspar had saved him from being held captive and tortured, he'd trained Kieran so Kieran would never again be a victim.

The Organization worked differently for the other agents. When the Walkers, humans and shifters had joined forces to protect innocents from their own kind, a declaration had been made. The first-born child in every family would be contracted to a lifelong service in the Organization. Just thinking about how Dakota and Remy had had no choice in their futures pissed him off. Remy might have accepted his fate, but at least he still had contact with his family and birth Pack. Dakota didn't. Once she'd been born and her parents had known she'd be sent off, they'd decided not to get attached to her.

Not get attached to their own child.

Dakota never spoke about her family and that was a good thing. If Kieran ever met the people who'd birthed her, he didn't know if he could keep control.

"Your hands are fisted and you're gritting your teeth," Remy said. "What the hell is going on?"

"Fuck!" Kieran ran his hands roughly over his face. He'd gotten lost in his thoughts again and he was supposed to be on patrol. "I'm just tired." He grasped at any excuse his partner might accept.

"And stressed," Remy added. "You're more worried about your father than you want to let on."

"True, but that's no excuse not to be on top of things. Sorry. Let's concentrate on finding us some wild animals," Kieran said.

"Yeah," Remy responded. "Because it can never be just a few stray dogs."

"Not with us," Kieran stated. He and Remy always got the weird cases. Speaking of cases, Kieran glanced around. "Where's the other team?" Caspar had given Kieran strict instructions not to fuck with the new agents. He was under orders to behave. It was as if Caspar didn't even know him sometimes. Of course Kieran was going to fuck with them.

Remy grinned.

"What'd you do?" There was a reason that Remy made the perfect partner for him. Dakota might believe that Kieran was a bad example, but the truth of the matter was Remy could be just as evil on his own.

"I might have suggested we meet in one of the small conference rooms to make a plan for the night."

Kieran laughed. "I bet a hundred bucks that they wait at least an hour before figuring out we aren't coming."

"An hour?" Remy pressed his lips together.

"At least."

"No way they'll wait that long," Remy stated. "You're on."

Kieran slapped his hands together before he rubbed them in glee. If Remy was on his side, they were going to have so much fun with the human and lion shifter.

"What's the address for the latest sighting?" Remy asked. "We might as well get some work done as we wait for the rookies."

"Maybe we'll even solve the case." Kieran flipped through the file that Remy had tossed onto the dash. "Remember that gas station that reported strange lights a few months back?"

"The store manager who'd been smoking meth?" Remy replied.

"Yeah."

"Please tell me we didn't take a fucking report from that asshole."

"No," Kieran said. "But the sighting was from the laundromat three stores down."

"Fine," Remy mumbled. Kieran bit back a grin. Remy had almost bitten off the head of the idiot who had reported a UFO above his shop. He'd been tripping and adamant about seeing the spaceship. "But if I run into that jackass, I'm not going to be nice."

Kieran laughed. "You're supposed to be the nice one. If you start acting like me, I don't know where my place is in this relationship."

Remy merely grunted in response.

Feeling better, Kieran gazed out of the window, looking for any signs of the wild animals that had been reported. He didn't think he'd find any. In his opinion, it was probably a bunch of young and drunk shifters that couldn't hold the transformation. Nobody had been hurt, so there was little suggestion that the shifters were trying to cause real trouble.

He hoped no one was injured accidentally, though. Since there'd been several sightings, the problem was not going away. They needed to get to the bottom of what was happening.

"Almost there," Remy told him.

"It's still early evening," Kieran said. "If they're coming from bars, we might not see anyone."

"What do you say we park and walk around? Test those superior senses of yours like Dean wants?" Remy suggested.

"I guess." Kieran knew that he needed to go into the lab and have his blood tested again. Since they'd learned that the shifters that'd held him for ten years had messed with his DNA, Dean had been helping Kieran to keep an eye on his abilities. He was more powerful than any of the Walkers he knew, so Kieran was certain something had been done to him. He just didn't know what.

"That's the spirit!" Remy teased.

"Just find a place to park," Kieran grumbled.

A couple of minutes later Remy pulled into the gravel parking lot of a local bar. "Let's check this place out. It shares an alley with the laundromat."

"Good idea," Kieran agreed. He waited until Remy had turned off the ignition before he pushed open the door.

The scents that assaulted him were not pleasant. Body odor, stale beer, urine and puke. "Jeez," he muttered.

"Even I can smell how bad it is," Remy said.

Beneath the recent smells, he could pick up the distinct stench of shifter. He didn't like the shifter aroma, with Dakota being the only exception. Even Remy had a whiff of wet dog to him. Dakota, though, just smelled like his. He concentrated and, as much as he didn't want to, Kieran breathed deeply to get a better idea of what they were dealing with.

"Bears," he said.

Remy stumbled on his way to the door. "Really? Damn it. They're unpredictable."

His partner was right about that. Grizzly bears, especially, were notorious for having a superior attitude toward other shifters but especially humans. "Let's take a look inside." With it still being early, hopefully whoever they ran into wasn't stupid drunk yet. But Kieran knew that his and Remy's luck never ran that good.

"Maybe we should have waited for the lion." Kieran led the way with Remy watching their back.

"Fucking cats," Remy spat.

"Ha!" Kieran pointed a finger at him.

Remy scowled back then grinned. "Oh yeah, you're fucking a cat."

"Shit." Kieran shuddered. "Not like that. I was just going to say I was telling Dakota on you."

"Whatever, man." Remy shrugged. "You're the one fucking the cat."

"Keep it up," Kieran threatened. "You haven't seen Dakota's claws yet." He pulled open the door and stepped inside.

The interior of the bar was dim, but Kieran had no trouble seeing. Right away he picked up the ruckus coming from the back corner. Over by the pool tables was a group of men, three huge bald guys with one skinny older man. It was the skinny older man who was practically yelling insults to what appeared to be several young human males at the bar.

Kieran turned his head toward his partner and noticed him discreetly stalking toward the bar. While Remy walked left, Kieran strolled to the right side of the room, which would take him past the pool tables. If these assholes wanted trouble, Kieran had no problem giving them what they wanted. *Damn shifters should know better.*

Out of the corner of his eye, he saw the bartender reach down and pull out a baseball bat. He laid it on a shelf behind him, putting it within easy reach. Yeah, Kieran was reading the room right. The group in the back had worn out their welcome. As Kieran got closer, he picked up the bear odor he'd recognized outside.

Remy gave him a hand signal that the rest of the room was made up of humans. That meant the baseball bat the bartender had wasn't going to do a bit of good against a group of shifters. It looked as though his and Remy's timing had been perfect.

One of the bigger guys with bright red hair noticed Kieran stalking closer and nudged the older skinny dude.

A cloudy alcohol-filled gaze met his. The skinny dude sneered.

Kieran wanted to laugh. He'd wipe that look off the dude's face quickly enough.

He was surprised when he finally reached the group and found the skinny dude wasn't a bear shifter like the others. *Some kind of bird.* Bears and bird shifter together—that was pretty unusual.

"Is there a problem here?" Kieran asked in a low, deep voice.

"None of your business, pretty boy," the skinny bird shifter responded. "Just keep walking."

Kieran turned to face the guy. "Now, I'd love to do that, but I figure as soon as I leave, you're going to start tearing up this place and put these humans in danger. I can't allow that."

His statement caught the bird shifter's attention. The bird shifter breathed in before he frowned. "What are you?"

"You don't want to find out. Why don't you go ahead and leave while you can still walk?" *Okay, that was a little over the top.* A little villain-sounding, but Kieran liked playing the role of the bad guy.

"You gonna make me?" the bird shifter asked as he took a step forward. He motioned for the three bear shifters to join him.

"If I have to," Kieran replied. "If I do, you'll be sleeping off your drunk in one of the cells in the basement of the Organization."

"Fuck!" The biggest of the bear shifters spat. No one wanted to come to the attention of the Organization. It showed the bear shifter had at least one ounce of smarts.

Kieran nodded. They knew he wasn't playing around now.

"And you and…" The bird shifter sniffed. "Your dog are the ones going to put us there?"

Kiran did smile this time, letting his fangs peek through his lips. "Yes," he hissed.

All four shifters took a step back. Now that was the respect he wanted. "Or you can leave now and not return to this establishment. You've worn out your welcome, as I said."

The big bear shifter grabbed the bird shifter's arm and pulled him back. "Come on, Carl. This place is dead, anyway."

"Fine." Carl turned around. "I was getting bored."

Kieran watched until every last man was out of the door.

The patrons in the bar began to applaud. Kieran took a bow. Then he headed to the bartender. "Did they have any open tab?"

"No," the bartender said. "I made them pay up front."

"Good man," Kieran praised. He pulled a card from his back pocket. "If they return or anyone gives you more trouble, just give me a call."

"Thanks." The bartender put the card under the cash register. "Can I get you gentlemen a drink?"

Kieran nodded to his partner for Remy to question the guy to see if he'd seen anything suspicious recently. Remy was better at talking to people.

As his partner was busy, Kieran decided to stroll back around and check the front to make sure those shifters were gone.

He peered out of the front glass and could have sworn someone or something darted back into the shadows. He narrowed his eyes but couldn't have said for sure he'd spotted anything.

Probably just jumpy after all the talk about my father earlier. He just needed to calm down. The fact that his father might or might not show up in his city was something that Kieran could not control. What Kieran could do, keep his new family safe, he would.

Kieran rolled his shoulders then turned back to listen in to what the bartender was saying to Remy. Yes, there has been more shifters around the area than usual. He hadn't had any trouble before that night, but there'd been some rumblings from others in the neighborhood. As Remy got a list of who he should be talking to, there was movement outside the front again. Yeah, he was certain he was being watched. Kieran had a pretty good idea about the culprit as well. He grinned, rolling to the balls of his feet. It had been a while since he'd had some good old-fashioned down and dirty fighting fun.

His partner joined him and Kieran nodded at the door. "We've got company."

Remy sneered. "I thought they left too easy."

"Wanna have some fun?" Kieran asked, hopeful.

"Like I'm going to tell you no," Remy replied. "But if you get hurt, Dakota is going to blame me. I just know it."

"Those fuckers aren't going to hurt me," Kieran said. "Come on! It's been forever since I've gotten to throw down."

"Fine, let's go."

Kieran followed Remy out, letting his partner take the lead. He wasn't surprised when Remy strolled casually toward the alley. If they wanted to keep Kieran's abilities hidden, it was better that they didn't have an audience.

A soft shuffle of feet was his only warning that they were being followed. Even a shifter wouldn't have been able to pick up the slight rustle of clothes. From Dean's testing, they'd figured that Kieran's hearing had been manipulated to give him about five times the ability of a shifter. They didn't know how, but the results were undeniable.

Anticipation and excitement grew as they walked behind the building. The street light was broken, but Kieran didn't need it. Neither would the shifters. Not that their sight was better than his — whatever had been done to him had amplified his eyesight as well.

"Hey, asshole!"

Kieran turned toward the mouth of the alley where the skinny bird shifter stood with his bear shifter companions. "Did you grow some balls?" Kieran taunted.

"Get him!" the bird shifter ordered.

Kieran caught the first fist that was directed at him before letting his fangs come down. "Let's party," he murmured. He might even allow Remy in on the fun.

Chapter Two

The drive out to the Red Rocks always took longer than Dakota liked being cooped up in a car. When Kieran drove her out there, with her clinging to his back on the bike, she felt free and excited. Now all she felt was anxious.

Gabe and Dare kept up a steady bout of conversation, but she didn't contribute much. Dakota hated being driven away from the city where she was certain Kieran would be finding trouble. He had a lot of excess energy he needed to burn off. She hoped he did so safely. But she knew her lover and the chances of him not ending up bloody by the end of the night were low. Hopefully Remy would be able to rein him in a little. Not that Remy was much better. Kieran liked to imply that Remy was a good influence, but she'd seen the wolf shifter pull some crazy stunts himself.

Finally, they reached their destination and Dakota let out a relieved sigh.

As much as she wanted to strip and transform into her jaguar, she had a job to do. She couldn't really question witnesses or take statements when she couldn't talk.

Gabe pulled the SUV up to where they were set to meet with the Alpha and sighed.

Dare grunted beside him. "This will be interesting."

Dakota held back a smile. Being one of the few shifters that wasn't intimated by the strong Alpha was a benefit in her line of work. Dakota respected Damon, but she didn't fear him. With all her experience with the Day Walker community, or Kieran specifically, it took a lot nowadays to frighten her. She danced with forces stronger than an Alpha wolf shifter. Kieran's cousins had been ruthless and intent on destroying what she and Kieran had built. Now with Kieran's father threatening to take him away from her, or worse, Dakota knew the upcoming fight would be epic.

The Alpha strolled forward into sight with two other wolves at his back, all in their shifter forms. She'd seen Damon transformed into his wolf form before but even if she hadn't, Dakota would have had no doubt which wolf he was. The power that surrounded the Alpha was felt even from inside the vehicle.

"Fuck," Gabe spat.

"Yeah." Dare was shivering. He was human, so the Alpha's influence shouldn't be affecting him as much as her and Gabe, since they were shifters.

There was an increase in the breeze. The wind batted against the SUV then the three wolf shifters changed back to human.

"I think we have clothes in the back," Dakota said. Not that she minded the three naked men standing outside the door, but she wasn't there to admire. She could do that secretly. Dakota loved Kieran, but she wasn't blind.

"I'll get them," Dare offered. He climbed out of the vehicle and Dakota followed suit. As Dare took care of passing out sweatpants, she peered around the area.

"It's so quiet out here," she said.

"The Pack enjoys the area." Damon stepped to her side. "You have an open invitation to shift here anytime you want."

She nodded. When Dakota transformed into her jaguar, she normally did so with Kieran. He'd been so against any kind of shifter that Dakota hadn't believed Kieran would want to see her transformed. Now that Dakota had all Kieran's trust and acceptance, she didn't want to run alone as her jaguar. Since he wasn't fond of other shifters still, she hadn't brought up wanting to transform inside the Pack security. That was asking too much.

"You can even bring your boyfriend," Damon muttered.

Dakota laughed. Kieran hadn't made it a secret that he didn't like shifters, with the exception of her and Remy. Damon hadn't gotten Kieran to add him to Kieran's small circle, although the Alpha was closer than he knew. Damon had helped them several times already, earning Kieran's trust. Dakota was letting the two men figure it out, though. For the time being, she'd just let Kieran and Damon circle each other until one of them offered a hand in friendship. It would happen, she hoped, sooner rather than later.

"Any unusual scents you or your Pack noticed?" Dakota asked.

"There're always new scents that belong to strangers. This area leads to a few of the harder hiking trails. It's why we don't come here often," Damon explained.

"How'd you find it?"

"One of my Pack members was bringing a guy up here for a day of hiking. After she stumbled on the ritual site, she called me," Damon said. "I came and saw for myself. It was creepy."

She'd seen the photos and agreed with his assessment. "I'll do some more digging on what the sigils mean."

Damon nodded. "I added more guards to try to stop anything like this happening again."

"I'm sure you'll do your best. The only way to be certain is to catch these people and stop them."

"We will." Damon gestured around. "This is my territory. My Pack's. I won't allow this to continue."

Dakota took his words as the threat they were. If she didn't find who was doing this before Damon did, then he'd take care of it himself. "Let me work this. I'll get to the bottom of it."

The Alpha turned. His eyes were bright. "Right now, they're sacrificing animals. How long until they capture a young or weak shifter? How long until we lose one of our own?"

He was right. "I know."

"Let's take a look around and then I'll accompany you to the other sites." Damon waved her forward.

"Sounds good." She took the first steps toward where Damon indicated. Dakota had a feeling the investigation wasn't going to be as simple as finding a few kids who hoped to summon a demon or talk to the devil.

The chill that traveled down her spine had been with her since she'd first heard about the case. This wouldn't be easy to solve.

The scent of old animal blood hit her before she stepped into the small cave. Most likely a house cat had been the victim. Dakota might be a deadly jaguar in her other form, but she was still sickened at what the poor cat had gone through.

Every protective instinct she possessed had to be tamped down before she roared in anger.

Damon clamped a hand on her shoulder.

Since felines were mostly solitary, she didn't have the same Pack instinct as some of the other shifters. That didn't mean the soothing presence of a strong Alpha didn't comfort her, though.

"It's harder seeing it in person," Damon murmured.

Yeah, it was. She'd thought she'd been prepared to be at the site, but the feeling of evil that remained shocked her. This wasn't kids, no, she was certain of that. The cold dread that had been building finally settled in the pit of her stomach.

"Have you ever seen these signs before?" she asked, walking to the wall. In addition to the pentagram that had been drawn in blood on the ground were the sigils on the walls. Okay, so more than one house cat. She'd have to check with Animal Control to see if any one area in the city was reporting more lost pets than the others.

"Only at the other sites," Damon answered.

"Hmm." She bent down to look at the way the floor had been cleaned. Had the culprits brought a fucking broom? The brush swipes in the dirt indicated they had. How screwed up was that?

Even though she had the photos from the file, Dakota took out her phone and snapped some for herself, including the way the dirt had been brushed aside. Once she had seen what she needed, she rose to her feet. Damon stood out of the way, at the entrance to the cave. She appreciated that he was letting them work.

Dare and Gabe were placing trace evidence into bags to take to their lab. The three of them had been working together long enough that they didn't even have to discuss who would do what part of the investigation.

"Almost done?" she called to her guys.

"Couple more minutes," Dare replied without looking up from scraping the blood from the wall.

Dakota didn't need to see any more so she strolled out of the cave and back into the fresh air. She couldn't get away from the bad feeling but at least she could breathe in something other than blood.

Damon followed her.

"Are the other sites the same?" she asked.

"Pretty much."

She nodded. They'd still have to check out each place to note any difference. Dakota wasn't looking forward to how her night was going to be spent.

* * * *

Kieran knew before he even set foot inside his suite that Dakota was already home. His side ached and there was blood on his clothes. She was going to be pissed. He couldn't avoid going inside, though. He needed to shower, change clothes then feed.

He slid the key card into the lock. The light flashed green and Kieran turned the knob before pushing the door open. One step inside.

"I smell blood."

Kieran lifted his head to see Dakota sprawled on the living room rug. She had file folders and pictures scattered around her while lying on her stomach. "Just a scratch."

She grunted. "I bet. Make sure you don't get blood on the carpet again. The housekeeping crew is going to quit if that keeps happening."

He stood above her, frowning. Dakota hadn't even looked up at him. Where was the concern? "Uh."

Laughing, she rolled over to peer up at him. "If you keep coming home bleeding, the novelty wears off."

Kieran narrowed his eyes. "Remy called you."

"Texted actually," she corrected. "He didn't want me mad at him."

"What about me?" Kieran groused. "*I* should be the one he's afraid of."

She smirked. "Pretty sure that ship sailed when he learned you had to have five thousand thread count sheets and twelve pillows on your bed to sleep."

"It's not twelve pillows," he grumbled. Kieran sulked as he made his way toward the bathroom to clean up. He passed his bed, disgusted to count that he did in fact have twelve pillows. Shit, Dakota was right. This was why he'd always held others at arm's length and hadn't shared his life with anyone. When he'd been stationed in Texas, neither Angel nor Remy had ever been to his residence. He'd kept his secrets. Now, after the years of striking fear in the heart of everyone he met, Kieran was losing that hold.

He resisted the urge to throw all the pillows at the wall and went into the bathroom instead. He turned on the shower, letting the dual water heads heat the small room.

All right, he liked his comforts. After being held and tortured for years, Kieran deserved to have the best his money could buy. That was all it was. He wasn't a snob or anything. He wasn't.

Damn, why was he letting Dakota's teasing get to him? He closed the bathroom door before tugging his shirt over his head. The claw mark on his side pulled, causing a hiss to escape, but he was already healing.

Once he had blood, there would be no mark on him at all.

Kieran finished undressing then stuck his hand into the water to check the temperature. Yes, he enjoyed scalding-hot showers as well. There was something about the cold that took him back to those long days where he hadn't known if he would see the next dawn.

"Stop it," he muttered. There was no reason for his thoughts to have gone so dark or back to the cell that'd once been his home. He had more than he could have ever hoped for. Being able to wake up every day with Dakota, working closely with his best friend and having the man who was like a father to him completed his life. That there were more people in his life like Jackson, Alex and Mitch was a bonus. Kieran should have been happy, not getting lost in memories that would only lead to pain.

He climbed into the shower, closing the glass door behind him, encasing himself in heat and steam. Kieran picked up the bar of soap and ran it over his wide chest. There were scars on his body, which was rare for a Walker. The years of abuse he'd suffered had left a mark on more than just his body, though. At times he felt as though his soul was marked.

The shower door opened behind him, but Kieran didn't turn. He'd heard Dakota enter the bathroom, the clothes dropping and her steady breath.

Kieran closed his eyes as her slick palms spread from his back to his stomach.

"You know I would have been worried if Remy hadn't already told me you were okay," she said. "I thought you'd be happy I didn't freak out."

"I am." He blew out a long breath. Kieran really was happy. He didn't want Dakota to worry about him.

"Then what's wrong?" Her lips trailed against the back of his neck.

"I don't know," he confessed. Kieran had been fine kicking ass and showing those assholes who was the boss. Then he'd headed home to Dakota. It wasn't until he'd set foot in the back door of the casino that it dawned on him he'd gone almost an hour without thinking about his father. That was when it had struck him that he could have been taken by surprise. He'd let his job and the thrill of the night keep him from being on guard. Not only could he have gotten himself killed, but Remy and Dakota as well. "Just in a mood."

"You can do better than that," she said. "Talk to me, please."

"I let myself forget."

She took the soap from his hands. Kieran leaned back as she took over cleaning his body. He kept his eyes closed to enjoy the attention. It was a reminder that he needed to keep sharp. He'd not let anything happen to Dakota. No, he'd die before Dakota was hurt.

He must have made some sort of sound that alerted her to his thoughts, because she dropped the soap before yanking him around.

"Look at me," she demanded.

Kieran opened his eyes.

Dakota cupped his face. "What did you forget?"

"That I have a target on my back," he whispered.

"Because of your father?"

"He's going to come," Kieran said. "He doesn't bluff."

"I'm not scared," she told him.

"I am," he admitted. "Terrified, like I haven't been since Caspar rescued me from hell."

She nodded. "Then it's a good thing that I'm here. And Caspar, Remy, Jackson and all the others."

"Our friends," he whispered.

"Our family," she said. "Yours and mine."

Kieran scoffed. "Neither one of us had any reason to believe in family."

"No, we don't," she agreed. "Or we didn't. But haven't the last few months shown us that we have people who care about us?"

They had. When his cousins had come to town, it had been agents, Jackson's people and even the Alpha who'd helped bring them down. Dakota was right. *Family.* The word had always made him sick. After being cast out of his clan, Kieran had never wanted to hear any association with the word *family* again. But that was what his little group had turned into.

"I'm an idiot," he muttered.

"Then you're my idiot," she teased. Dakota lifted to the tips of her toes and kissed him. "And I'm not going to let your father or anyone hurt our family."

"I won't either," he vowed.

"Good. Now why don't you show me that you're really okay?"

He grinned then pushed her back against the tile. Kieran dropped to his knees, which had the water hitting his shoulders and side. Ignoring the sting where the claw marks were slowly healing, Kieran ran his hands up her inner thighs. "Let me taste what's mine first."

"Yeah." She breathed heavily already but widened her stance.

Kieran lifted her left foot, guiding it to his shoulder.

"Please," she begged.

He trailed his fingers through her slick folds before leaning in and inhaling her sweet arousal. Kieran flicked out his tongue and tasted her just like he'd asked.

Dakota moaned then gripped the back of his head. She pushed him into her harder. Kieran used his tongue and fingers to bring her pleasure. Each time she cried out, Kieran was spurred on harder. He loved claiming her body as his. He might not have been a shifter, but he held the same urge to let others know she was marked.

Being a Walker gave him no scent. It was the absence of any smell that made him so different from humans and shifters. Humans picked up the odors of the places they'd been and what they'd touched. Day Walkers' bodies never held a trace of anything. He wished she could wear his scent but, her being unable to, he wanted Dakota to give off the aroma of *taken*. Her happiness, satisfaction and contentment worked to claim her. At least to the paranormal world.

"K!" she shrieked as her orgasm slammed through her.

He had to reach out and catch her so she didn't fall. Her legs shook as he stood with her in his arms. Kieran quickly turned off the water before stepping out of the shower.

Dakota snagged a towel off the warmer and ran it over his shoulders as he carried her into the bedroom. He laid her down on the mattress, following to cover her body with his.

"Inside me," she demanded.

Kieran climbed to his knees, spreading her thighs before gripping the base of his cock. He gave himself a few strokes as her gaze followed the movement. He loved teasing her, but he couldn't hold back much longer. He ached to fill her again.

"Kieran," she whined.

"Keep your eyes on mine," he ordered.

She looked up at him. Kieran would never get tired of the love and trust he saw in her eyes.

He pushed in the tip of his shaft before pausing.

"Take me," she said. "Claim me."

Kieran slid the rest of the way inside her slick pussy. He groaned as she clamped her inner muscles down on his cock.

He pulled back slowly before plunging in.

"Mine." He snarled the word. Kieran set up a steady pace, pumping his hips and driving deep into her.

Dakota held on to his shoulders, but never let her gaze slide from him.

The connection between them was strong and the spark that linked them flared. There was electricity in the air surrounding him. There were times when they made love and everything remained normal. Other instances, like tonight, the fire that ran from her to him almost consumed him. He needed so much.

"More! Please, I'm almost there," she yelled.

Kieran increased his thrusts until she screamed and climaxed. He slowed down when she collapsed onto the bed. He continued with lazy strokes until he came inside her.

Dakota wrapped her arms around his shoulders before sighing with pleasure.

"Good?" he asked. Not that he needed validation, but he couldn't resist.

"The best," she murmured and closed her eyes.

* * * *

Kieran picked up an extremely disturbing photo from the pile that Dakota had left on the floor. There was something about the words written on the cave wall that struck a familiar chord with him. He just couldn't remember where he might have seen them before.

"Every one of the sites had that one drawing on the wall," Dakota said as she walked into the living room. She'd pulled on a pair of cotton pajama bottoms and a tank top while he merely wore sweatpants.

"There's something…" He tapped the photo against his lips.

"What?" she asked.

He'd seen it somewhere but where? Kieran tried to rack his brain, but it wasn't coming to him. He strolled over to the desk where he had a laptop that was connected to the Organization's database. He pressed the power button then set the picture down on the desk.

"Kieran?"

He glanced over at his shoulder. "Yes?"

"What are you doing?"

"This symbol is familiar. I'm trying to remember from where," he explained.

"Okay," she said.

"I'm going to put it into the database we keep and see what comes up," he told her.

"I already did that," she said.

"But I'm concentrating on my cases. That will cut back the amount of data you'll have to sort through."

"Sounds good." She ran her hand down his back. "You need to get the search started then go feed."

It would be best. He couldn't afford to be weak. At any moment his father might show up and Kieran would have to fight. "I will."

"And take Jackson with you," she said.

Kieran frowned. "Why?"

"You know why," she responded.

"I don't need a babysitter," he said with a growl.

Dakota slid up next to him before turning and hopping on the only open space left on the desk. She kicked her legs while smiling.

"What?" He scowled.

"You're sexy when you're cranky."

"I'm not cranky."

"Are so," she singsonged. "Besides, you can ask Jackson if he recognizes the symbol. Isn't he like a billion years old? He might know."

Kieran barked out a laugh. "He's not a billion years old, but I'll tell him you think that."

"Go ahead," she replied. "I'm not afraid."

"Fine," Kieran agreed. He snapped a picture of the photo then transferred the image from his phone to his computer. As he worked on setting up the search, Dakota watched him.

"Don't you have work to do?" he asked. Dakota was always working. It wasn't like her to hover.

"Yep."

He completed the command for the computer to run then stepped back.

"Now go," she ordered.

Kieran narrowed his eyes at her. If she was up to something, it wouldn't bode well for him.

Dakota laughed. "I just want you strong. I ordered dinner for an hour and a half. Be back here? Please."

"Fine." He gripped the front of her tank, yanking her forward, to kiss her deeply.

Dakota was panting by the time he released her. "Damn," she managed.

"Just wanted to make sure you didn't get any ideas while I'm gone."

"Oh, I have all kinds of ideas," she practically purred. "I called Jackson for you as well. He's meeting you by the back door."

Damn, how long had he been staring at the photo? "Think you're sneaky, don't you?"

"I learned from the best."

God, she turned him on. He stepped between her legs before running his palms up her thighs.

His cell phone dinged.

"That's probably Jackson," she told him.

"I guess I should be going then." He kissed her one last time.

"Wear shoes!" she called out. "It looks weird when you don't."

"I'll wear shoes," he conceded.

"And a shirt!"

Kieran laughed. "And a shirt." Luckily a pair of sneakers and a T-shirt had been left on the couch. He gave the shirt a quick sniff and found it clean enough. He was probably going to get blood on it anyway. Not his blood, this time, at least.

Dakota was dropping back down to the carpet when he glanced over his shoulder at her. Okay, if she was getting back to work, that meant he had nothing to worry about. She'd just been taking care of him. Always worrying even when she tried to play down her concerns.

He took the elevator to the lobby.

"About time you showed up," Jackson quipped.

Kieran smirked at his oldest friend. They'd gone through hell together. Literally. Jackson was the only person who truly understood what Kieran had gone through in the ten years he'd been held by the shifters and experimented on. Jackson had been in the cage right next to him. "Had to give a proper goodbye to Dakota."

Jackson narrowed his eyes. "I hate you."

"No, you don't." Kieran smacked Jackson on the back as he turned serious. "Keep a lookout for anything. I don't believe my father will approach until he's gotten to see me with his own eyes. He never did trust others to report back as they should."

"Your father won't touch you," Jackson promised.

Kieran nodded. "Just don't want to be followed."

"I sent Alex and a few of my men to patrol around the streets before you came down. They'll keep a watch out as well."

Damn, Kieran really did owe a lot to Jackson. Not only had he sold Kieran the hotel suite for far less than he should have, but Jackson always had his back. Kieran had given real consideration to accepting Jackson's offer to join his security team, but Kieran couldn't leave Dakota. They might not work the same cases, but he at least knew what she was up to. If he left the Organization, he wouldn't have the same opportunity. Since Dakota would never be able to leave the group, Kieran was staying as well.

"Thank you," he said with sincerity.

"Anytime," Jackson replied. "Ready?"

"I've become a bad influence on you," Kieran stated as he led the way out of the door. The back of the hotel faced the six-level parking garage. The neighborhood located behind them was old but clean. Still, Kieran could usually find someone around who was up to no good. "You used to use donors only, before I moved in."

Jackson stayed walking by his side. "It is safer. But not nearly as fun."

"I bet this drives Alex crazy."

"Oh yeah," Jackson agreed with a grin. "I just remind him that it's good training to remain sharp." Jackson's head of security didn't need more training. Alex was good at having Jackson's back. But whatever worked. Kieran enjoyed hanging out with Jackson.

The farther they moved from the hotel, the darker the streets got. This part of the Strip wasn't where most tourists would be found. The houses and apartment buildings were for the residents who worked in the area. Kieran liked knowing he was keeping those people safe by hunting.

When he fed, the results for the chosen prey weren't pretty. Kieran only needed a few sips. He never drained someone. It was nearly impossible for a Walker to drain a body. That much blood wouldn't be good for the Walker. While it could be hard to stop drinking due to the instant warmth that filled him, Kieran had only needed to feed too much one time and get sick to learn his lesson. But his bite did make the person he fed from ill. If the person was human, they'd end up with flu-like symptoms. Shifters usually only got a headache. But that was why he didn't feed from Dakota. He would never harm her, not even giving her a headache. He'd given in and showed her the results of feeding and she hadn't complained but had been disappointed when it wasn't erotic like books and movies showed.

"Let's head east." Jackson read his phone. "Alex said there's more people that way."

Kieran took a right so they could cut across an alley. He wasn't getting the feeling that he was being followed so he had to wonder what his father was up to. The two weeks he'd been given to return home had expired. His father had to have known Kieran wouldn't go home on his own, so there had probably been a plan in place to retrieve him before Kieran had even hung up the phone. The problem was that since Kieran had been sent away at eighteen, he didn't know what his father would do. Or how he planned to get his way.

They walked down empty blocks, not coming across anyone. Kieran hated having to feed from someone who didn't deserve the illness they'd feel. Usually when he couldn't find prey, he paid one of the homeless or street worker to let him drink. They needed the money and at least Kieran didn't harm them permanently.

"We can go back to the hotel and use one of my donors," Jackson suggested.

Kieran disliked that even more. He understood the humans who Jackson kept on staff to feed from, but that didn't give him any enjoyment. He liked the chase and fight when he picked a mugger or thug.

Glancing at his watch showed him that thirty minutes had passed. Dakota had given him enough time that he could search a little more. "Not yet."

Jackson didn't seem to mind. He shot off a quick text before pocketing his phone.

They were coming up to one of the bars the locals seemed to favor. Jackson had caught a few people there who had needed to learn a lesson. Even as that thought struck Kieran, he spotted a man trying to stumble to an old beat-up truck. A woman was holding on to his arm, but neither human could walk a straight line. She was urging her man to hurry up so they could stop at the liquor store before it closed. *Like either of them needs more alcohol.*

"Ten o'clock," Kieran murmured.

"The drunk couple?" Jackson asked with a frown.

"They shouldn't be driving," Jackson said. "They've drunk too much. They could kill someone."

Jackson's features changed to a smile. "That's true. We'll be doing a public service getting them off the street."

"Plus they're so fucked up, they won't remember much."

"True," Jackson agreed. He was the one who had to worry about being recognized. The shifters might be out to the public, but no one knew about Day Walkers yet—at least no one who acknowledged it publicly. With the shifters outing themselves, there was still too much unease, so that showing the world Walkers or vampires existed would just be too much for humankind.

Jackson showed a rich and powerful façade to the public, making him well-known. He also monitored all supernatural types that entered his city. *That* he didn't share with the public. But his face was known for giving so much money to the city of sin. That popularity was why he'd been using donors to feed for so long. That and the fact that Jackson had grown bored with life before Kieran had shown up in town.

"I'll take the male, you take the female," Kieran told him.

"Got it." Jackson slowed and Kieran matched his stride. It was time to put his acting skills to the test, although Kieran wouldn't mind if the male fought back.

"Hey! Another bar!" Kieran slurred. "Let's get a drink." He made sure to speak loud enough that the humans would hear.

"Ah, man." Jackson played along. "I'm almost out of money." He pulled a fist full of bills from his pocket. "You think this is enough?" Jackson stumbled and let a few of the bills fall. Predictably, the humans stopped to look at them, their gazes going from the money in Jackson's hand to what he'd dropped.

"Fuck," Kieran drawled. "I think I got some." He yanked out a twenty-dollar bill from his own pocket.

He held it up close to his face as though he was having trouble reading it.

The human man pushed his partner against the truck before zeroing in on him and Jackson. Kieran made sure to drag his feet, kicking up dirt. He waved the twenty around.

"This has gotta be enough," Kieran said happily. Then tripped himself so he face-planted. He was good enough that he landed without hurting himself.

"Hey, buddy," the human male said. "You okay?"

Kieran rolled onto his back. Jackson kept walking toward the female, mumbling to himself about tequila, and acting as if he hadn't seen Kieran's fall.

"How'd I get down here?" Kieran asked the human man.

The guy crouched over him. "I think you fell."

"Nuh-uh," Kieran slurred. "No way."

The human reached out to help him up, smoothly taking the twenty from Kieran's hand, and pocketing it in the process. Oh yeah, this guy would make a good target. Kieran allowed the human male to haul him back to his feet. The human wrapped his arm around Kieran's back in the guise of holding him steady. He was also trying to get Kieran's wallet from his pocket. Damn this guy wasn't very good at pick-pocketing. Kieran was wearing sweats. He could feel every move the guy was making.

From the direction of the female and Jackson, he heard a squeak. The human man turned his head to check on his girlfriend or whoever she was and that was when Kieran struck.

He bit down hard on the man's neck, allowing his fangs to tear cleanly through the soft flesh.

Warmth flooded his body as the first taste of blood hit his tongue.

The man tried to bring his arms up, but Kieran easily pinned him and drank deeply for a few sips before he pulled away.

"Now let's talk about all the things you did wrong tonight and how you're going to change your ways," Kieran told the human.

Chapter Three

The lack of information about the sigil and marking was giving Dakota a headache. She'd been researching for hours now and didn't feel as though she was making any progress. Even with Kieran's search, she wasn't finding what she needed.

She groaned while stretching out her back. Dakota knew she should have moved to the desk or table, but she liked being able to spread out. The number of papers had doubled from when Kieran had left, but none of it was helping her figure out who could be behind the rituals in the Red Rock area.

The soft knock on the suite door was a welcome distraction. She glanced at the clock in the corner of her laptop screen. It wouldn't be the food yet, so she cautiously crept to the door. Surely Kieran's father wouldn't just show up to the suite. Plus they'd given security a picture of the Elder Argent, so the security system, with its face recognition software, would pick him up if he entered the casino.

Dakota peered through the peephole of the door and sighed. *Damn it, what did Kieran do now?*

She opened the door and glared at the two men who stood in the hall. "You're not my dinner," she said. "But you could be if you're here to make trouble."

Caden, the young lion shifter, took a step back. Yeah, Dakota could take him in both human and shifter form. James merely smirked at her while not moving at all.

"I heard you were just as fierce as your boyfriend," James said.

"You should listen to the rumors," she responded. Dakota didn't know what Kieran had done that had the two agents showing up, but it couldn't be good. Still she wouldn't allow anyone to fuck with her lover.

"Is he here?" James asked. "I called Remy and he said that he'd dropped Kieran off to change clothes. Guess they were a little bloody."

She narrowed her eyes. "And where were you when my boyfriend and his partner were taking on three bear shifters and a bird shifter?"

James laughed. "We were ditched and trying to find them. Caspar suggested putting a GPS tracker on them, but we thought he was kidding."

Okay, Dakota wasn't surprised at all. She opened the door wider. "Come in. Kieran stepped out for a minute, but he'll be right back." It was still technically the middle of their shift so it wasn't like the agents were out of line showing up there when Kieran and Remy weren't in the field.

The Organization ran differently from other companies. While they might technically be on company time from seven p.m. to seven a.m., they didn't clock in and out. There were too many times they worked other hours during investigations. The monthly salary the agents were paid was huge, but they earned every penny they got.

Caden peered around the suite with a look of awe on his face. James, being the more experienced partner, was moving toward the research on the carpet. "You're working the ritual case, right?" James asked.

"Don't mess up my piles," she warned.

James stuck his hands into the pockets of his suit. Hell, who wore suits when working for the Organization? They needed to blend in. He was eyeing some of the photos spread out.

"And yes, that's the case I'm working." She closed the hotel door, hoping that Kieran wouldn't be much longer. She didn't like strangers in their private space, getting their scents on their belongings. She knew it was a possessive shifter trait, but she didn't care. "You want a drink while you wait?" They didn't use the kitchen for much, but she could offer beverages.

"Water?" James asked.

"Sure." She turned to Caden, who still looked like he might swallow his tongue. Jeez, had she been that green when she'd gotten out of training? Dakota couldn't remember ever being that innocent.

"Could I have a Coke please, if you have one?" Caden asked.

"You got it." Remy and Mitch were the only ones who drank Coke, but Dakota and Kieran kept some stocked for that reason.

She strolled to the kitchen while keeping an eye on James to make sure he wasn't touching any of her work. By the time she was walking back into the living room, Kieran opened the door and entered. Dakota sighed in relief.

Kieran stopped in the entry before glaring at their guests. "What the fuck do you two want?" he growled.

Caden jumped from where he'd been looking out of the large windows overseeing the Strip.

"Came to meet up with our partner for the case," James quipped.

"You are not my partner," Kieran declared. He stomped in the room, not slowing down until he spotted Dakota. He relaxed visibly before her eyes.

"Hey," she murmured, sliding closer to him. "You look better."

He gave her a sharp nod before taking the drinks from her hands. Kieran handed the Coke to Caden before he stalked to James. How he knew who had requested what drink, Dakota didn't know. She'd have to ask him later.

Kieran tossed the bottle of water to James, making him have to reach out to catch it. Luckily he did. Dakota would have been pissed off if the bottle had fallen on top of her work. "I'm working from here for the rest of the night," Kieran said. "You're not needed."

James shrugged before he twisted the lid off the top of the bottle of water. "We're here, so we might as well help. Where were you just now?"

Kieran's growl sent a shiver down Dakota's spine. And it wasn't from fear. Poor Caden paled, though, so she knew she needed to defuse the situation fast. James should not be questioning Kieran. *Does the man have a death wish?*

"Look," James said, "Remy already filled us in about the bar and what happened. We drove around the area ourselves—while looking for you two, I might add—and didn't see any trouble. I was just wondering if you were out patrolling on your own. If we should add this area to our rotation."

"There was no trouble around here," Kieran said, without answering James' question.

"If the cops get any calls about wild animals, they'll be directed to us," James said. "I also have a buddy who works for Animal Control and I told him to give me a ring if he hears anything, too."

Kieran had his lips pressed tightly together, but at least he was listening to James.

"How do you have a buddy working for the city already?" Kieran questioned.

"Is this the getting-to-know-you part of our relationship?" James responded. "Want to know my favorite color?"

"Shit," Dakota muttered. Kieran was going to kill the stupid human if he kept smarting off.

"Christ," Kieran said. "Answer the fucking question and I'll think about letting you work with me."

"I'm pretty sure we were ordered to work with you," James pointed out.

"How's that working out for you?" Kieran asked.

James barked out a laugh. It made the agent appear younger. "God, you really are an ass."

Kieran shrugged.

"But you're also the best agent we have in the city. I met Adam, my friend from Animal Control, at a bar. I took him home and fucked him. Found out later what he did for a living. That enough info for you?" James crossed his arms over his chest defensively.

Kieran opened his mouth and Dakota knew what he was going to ask.

"Don't you dare!" she called to him.

He turned to look at her. "What?"

"It's not any of your business if James' friend is good in bed."

Kieran's wide smile told her that was exactly the question he'd been going to ask. "Fine." He turned back toward James. "I guess you can help."

"Thanks for your consent," James responded. "Do I need a permission slip to take a piss?"

"If it's in the middle of a fight, then yes," Kieran replied easily.

James rolled his eyes then glanced back down at the photos he'd remained standing by. "Mind if I pick this up?" he asked her.

Dakota nodded. She was curious why he was so interested in her case.

He crouched down before choosing the photo of the brush marks she'd taken from her phone. "They swept the cave first."

So she wasn't the only one who found that tidbit weird. "Yeah."

"Huh," he said. "That adds an even bigger creepy factor."

"I know, right?" she agreed.

"Food's here," Kieran interrupted. James and Caden glanced at the door, which no one had knocked at.

Dakota was used to Kieran hearing the elevator and the cart being rolled to their suite. She crossed the room and had the door open seconds after the hotel employee knocked.

It only took a few moments to get their dinner set up and the employee to leave.

"We'll take off, so you can enjoy your food in peace. But please call if you get a lead on our case." James passed Kieran a card.

Kieran accepted the small rectangle of paper before slipping it into his pocket. "See you at the office."

"Sure thing." James motioned to Caden to follow him.

"And, James?" Kieran called out before the human agent could open the door.

"Yeah?" James didn't even turn around.

"Wear jeans tomorrow," Kieran ordered.

James shook his head. "I look damn good in my suits."

Dakota waited until James and Caden had left and the door behind them was closed before walking to the table. "I don't know what I think about those two."

"James is a good agent. He'll be an asset to the office," Kieran said. He already had the dome off his dish and was pulling the plate filled with the steak, potatoes and vegetables to him.

"Sit down and eat," she ordered. "You don't need to stand over your laptop and watch the search run."

He chuckled but complied. Dakota sat across from him. "How do you know that James is a good agent?" There was no way that Kieran had had time to run a search on the agents. Hell, he'd probably talked someone into doing it for him.

"Caspar told me," Kieran said around a mouthful of rare steak.

She should have known. Caspar wasn't going to assign Kieran anyone the boss wasn't one hundred percent sure of. "And Caden? I don't think I've heard him say one word."

"He scored the highest from his group in his training class, but that doesn't mean it'll transfer over to real life. Caspar wants to make sure he doesn't get himself killed in his first month," Kieran shared.

"And he put him with you?" Dakota was starting to doubt their boss' sanity.

"Trial by fire," Kieran told her. "If he's not going to be able to hack it in Vegas, Caspar needs to know now if he needs to be transferred to another division."

Yep, Caspar was losing his mind. Kieran was the worst choice to evaluate a shifter. "He could have been put with my team. We're uneven with three when most teams are just two people."

Kieran shrugged. "Do you want a new partner?"

When Dakota had been assigned to the Vegas office, she'd been partnered up with Caspar's nephew, Dean. The two of them had worked for years as the top field team until Dean had decided to follow his true passion and been asked to be put in the lab. Dean had hated field work while Dakota thrived on the investigations.

Since Gabe and Dare had been the team that had backed them up the most, she'd been put with them after Dean had moved to the lab. She liked both Gabe and Dare, but she wasn't as close to them as she had been to Dean. Before she'd met Kieran, Dean had been her best friend. Now she only saw him once a week or so. They worked different shifts, so it was hard to line up any time to see each other.

"A new partner? I don't know." Dakota hadn't really thought about it. She was just wondering about the new agents while talking out loud.

"I'm pretty sure that it's my fault you don't have a new partner," Kieran told her.

Dakota paused with her fork full of lasagne halfway to her mouth. "Explain."

"He knows that if he sticks you with a partner who puts you in danger, I'm likely to kill them," Kieran answered. He never stopped shoving his food in his mouth as he talked. Dakota frowned. He shouldn't be that hungry. Hadn't he eaten that day. *Wait, what?* "What?"

Kieran finally looked up. "If you got hurt because your partner was stupid, I'd kill your partner. That would probably lead to a whole bunch of paperwork that I wouldn't want to do. Then Caspar would have to nag me to do the paperwork. It would become a whole thing." He waved his hand.

For a brief moment, Dakota had absolutely no idea how to respond to Kieran's statement. The way he spoke, so casually, about killing another agent should have scared her. "You... I..." She dropped her fork. "You already threatened Caspar with that!" she accused. Holy shit, she knew that Kieran was different from other agents, but this was over the top even for him.

"I didn't threaten," Kieran defended himself. "I merely informed our boss what would happen if you were hurt in the field."

"What about Dare and Gabe?" she asked.

Kieran tore into a hot roll before he began to butter it. "They've proven that they have more than half a brain. They're okay, for now."

"Okay for now," she repeated. Dakota sat back and watched her lover as he stuffed half the roll in his mouth. This was outrageous and yet she wasn't mad. Maybe Kieran was starting to rub off on her just a little too much.

There was a beep from the laptop and she jumped up. She needed to think about sacrifices and blood and weird symbols. That she could deal with. Kieran's declaration needed to be pushed to the back of her mind. *Way back.* Jeez, they were a screwed-up couple if he went around killing people who caused her to get hurt and she was turned on by that fact.

Kieran's laptop screen was blinking with the notification that a result had been found.

"What is it?" he asked. He hadn't slowed down one bit.

"Jeez, didn't you eat earlier?" she questioned.

"Forgot," Kieran said. "We got in a fight, drove around looking for wild dogs, visited, like, twenty bars then had to chase down a purse snatcher. When Remy wanted to get dinner, I had him drop me off here to change clothes instead. I was all dirty. I don't like to eat food when I'm all dirty. You know that."

"Yeah, sure." She was only half-listening to Kieran's explanation. The report that she'd clicked on already had her complete attention. It hadn't actually been Kieran's case but one that he'd come into later after a couple of agents had gone missing.

"What's wrong?"

Dakota jumped, not having realized that Kieran was up from the table and standing behind her.

He slid his palm down her back, soothing her.

She hit Print so she could read the entire report without answering him. He was reading over her shoulder, anyway.

"This was years ago," Kieran murmured. "Right after I came out of training. Remy hadn't even been assigned to me yet. I think Angel did most of the research while I tried to find any trace of the agents. I don't remember much of it."

Could it be a copy-cat or something more sinister going on?

As soon as the printer finished spitting out the pages she needed, she grabbed them then moved to the couch. She read as Kieran used the laptop to refresh his memory of the case.

Halfway through the first page, Dakota was glad she hadn't gotten more than a couple of bites down. Her stomach roiled as the gruesome details of the murdered agents were revealed. Whoever had written the report hadn't spared any detail.

"Jesus Christ," she muttered. "This is bad… Really bad." There were too many similarities between Kieran's early case and what was currently happening. She needed to call Caspar. She had to warn Damon. This was going to be a fucking mess.

* * * *

Kieran didn't like it when Dakota left for early morning meetings. They were supposed to be tucked away in bed with her in his arms, the mountain of blankets and pillows comforting them as they peacefully dreamed.

Instead of sleeping, Dakota had run around like a madwoman, organizing meetings and putting together reports of what she suspected. Kieran couldn't sleep without her, which meant that at nine in the morning, he was wandering around on the bottom floor of the casino. He didn't gamble, hated crowds and didn't have anything better to do.

He reached out and grabbed the hand that nearly touched his shoulder. Just because he was tired didn't mean he'd let his guard down. Kieran squeezed the slim wrist in his hold.

"You could break my wrist and I still wouldn't utter a sound," Alex growled into his ear.

"I should, I really should," Kieran threatened. "And you should know better than to come up behind me." He let go of Alex.

"I actually thought I had a chance of sneaking up on you," Alex told him. He strolled forward until he stood before Kieran.

That comment from anyone else would have been hilarious, but Alex meant it. He'd been working hard to hone his skills after finding out how powerful Kieran was. Alex didn't like knowing there was anyone out there stronger than him or Jackson. Alex's entire life was dedicated to protecting Jackson. If Kieran hadn't been a friend, then he would have been a real danger.

Knowing that he'd never beat Kieran using his Walker powers, Alex had begun to learn what he could improve. He'd even gone through some sort of Navy Seal training.

"Right before you went to grab me, you shuffled your feet," Kieran told him, hoping to be helpful.

"Really?" Alex frowned. "I didn't know I did that."

"You were adjusting your stance to be able to make the grab," Kieran said. "If I'd been anyone other than me, you'd have succeeded."

Alex nodded, obviously paying close attention to Kieran's advice.

"Stop hesitating," Kieran said. "Think about what you want to do then do it."

"Okay." Alex glanced around. "Where's Dakota? Why are you even awake right now?"

"She had to go into the office," Kieran answered.

"And she left you here on your own?" Alex questioned. "Does she hate me?"

"I promised her I'd stay out of trouble," Kieran offered.

"That's why you're prowling like a caged lion?"

Kieran scoffed. "I don't prowl. I think I'm offended by that."

Alex nudged Kieran out of the walkway toward the coffee shop. "Let me buy you a drink. Then I need to get some last-minute work done before I head to bed myself."

"Fine," he agreed, following Alex. He did like the coffee down there. After he finished his coffee he was going to go back the suite so no one else could accuse him of looking for trouble. Luckily the line was short and he soon had a steaming cup of house brew in his hand.

Alex's phone chimed and Kieran waved him off even before Alex started to make his excuses to having to leave. It wasn't easy being head of security for the empire that Jackson had created. There was even less time for Alex to have any kind of life than it was for agents working with the Organization. Kieran was going to have to remind Jackson again that Alex needed time off.

Alex hurried away with one hand holding his cup and the other up to his ear as he barked orders into the phone. Someone was in trouble. Kieran settled himself into a small table located in the corner. He could see the entire entrance and all the other patrons from his seat.

He narrowed his gaze at the young woman who was openly staring at him.

Usually just the sight of Kieran was enough to have a stranger scurrying away, especially when he scowled, like he was now.

The young lady smiled.

What in the hell is wrong with her?

He had a wall at his back and no one could come up behind him. That didn't stop his urge to look over his shoulder to see who she might be pleased to see. He resisted, barely, and picked up his coffee to ignore her. Maybe if he pretended she wasn't there, she'd stop.

Less than three minutes later, the girl was standing next to his table.

"Go away," Kieran growled.

"I'm Kayla," she responded.

"Don't care," he replied.

"No, you're supposed to say it's nice to meet me," she told him. "Ask me to sit with you."

"You're way too young for me," he said. "Are you even old enough to be in the casino? Why don't you go talk to the barista?" Kieran waved to the college-aged kid behind the counter.

"But I want to talk to you, Kieran."

He straightened. "I didn't tell you my name." Kieran was suspicious now. Was this one of his father's spies? His father couldn't get into the hotel without being recognized so he'd sent this girl? He took a deep breath and pulled in the same familiar scent as his mate. That couldn't be right. There were differences, but this girl was a jaguar shifter.

She sat down and peered at him. "Put it together yet?" she asked.

His mind still on his father, Kieran was ready to do battle.

"I don't need you to tell me your name because everyone here knows it. And Dakota's. When I saw my aunt with you, I was intrigued. I can't scent you so I find that strange but maybe it's an agent thing..."

Kieran's mind was spinning with all the words the girl spewed. Aunt, lack of scent—what the hell was going on?

"Listen, little girl—"

"My name's Kayla," she replied patiently. "I'm your girlfriend's niece. I came to meet the aunt who's never been around."

"That's not her fault. You should go home before you get involved in things that you have no business knowing about," he advised. Kieran wasn't sure how Dakota would take the sudden appearance of her niece. Did Dakota even know she had one? Probably. Kieran just wasn't certain how close tabs she kept on her family.

"Like the Organization?" Kayla asked.

Kieran didn't respond. He darted his gaze around to make sure that no one was paying attention.

Kayla leaned forward. "You work there too?" Kayla sounded excited. "I tried to ask my dad about it, but he didn't know anything. He said they don't ever talk about it."

"And yet you seem to know," Kieran pointed out.

"My favorite cousin was first born. He told me that he'd be leaving when he was ten. I was eight. He told me what he knew, but a ten-year-old doesn't really explain the way things work too well. After Greg left, I found some journals in my grandpa's library from an ancestor who was one of the first agents in our family."

Kieran nodded to encourage Kayla to keep talking. He'd been hesitant to ask Dakota about her family and this was free information. He still didn't know how he was going to tell Dakota that her long-lost niece had shown up, but he'd worry about that later.

"I've tried to contact Greg, but he'd been in some kind of school that wouldn't allow me to talk to him and now he lives in London," Kayla told him. "I went through the ledger and found Dakota's name. It's taken me a couple of years to track down where she is but I finally got a lead when I saw a news report with her name on it. She looks just like my grandma and I knew she was my family."

"How old are you?" he asked.

"I turned eighteen over the summer," Kayla replied.

Jeez, so young. "And where do your parents think you are?" There was no way Dakota's family was aware that Kayla was tracking her down.

Kayla shrugged. "On a road trip for with some friends. It's supposed to be my high school graduation present."

"You should get back on the road and take that trip," Kieran advised her.

The way Kayla slumped and crossed her arms over her chest really did show how young she was. "I want to talk to my aunt."

There was no good option here. Kayla wouldn't leave until she'd met Dakota and Dakota wouldn't be able to give Kayla the answers she was seeking. "I don't think that's a good idea."

"I just want you to introduce me," Kayla said. "I tried to walk up and just talk to her, but I chickened out. Does she even know she has a niece? Or nephews? My brother doesn't remember much about her."

"I can…talk to her for you," Kieran offered. "But I'm not making any promises."

Kayla bounced in her chair. "You will?"

"That doesn't mean she'll want to see you," Kieran reminded her. He didn't want to hurt the child, but what Kayla was doing would get her in a lot of trouble. He honestly couldn't say what Dakota would do, but reporting her niece was a good possibility. Dakota was a true agent. "Where are you staying?"

"My friends and I have a small vacation house north of here," she said. "We thought it would be easier than staying in a hotel. We can't get into the casinos anyway."

"Okay. Give me your number and I'll give you a call after I talk to Dakota."

Kayla excitedly wrote her number on a napkin with the coffee shop logo before shoving it at him. "Thank you!" She raced around the table and hugged his neck before he could stop her. No one touched Kieran. *Ever.* He wasn't even sure how to respond.

Luckily, as quickly as she'd hugged him, she was letting go.

"I'll wait for your call," Kayla said before scurrying away, leaving Kieran to question what he'd offered. He needed to find a way to talk to Dakota and keep her calm. He really couldn't see this situation going well. And he couldn't blame Dakota one bit.

She'd been marked from the second she'd been brought into the world. There'd been no doubt about what her future held. Dakota's legacy had been determined centuries ago.

He'd once asked Dakota what she would have done if she'd been given a choice. She'd peered at him in confusion before admitting she'd never thought about it because it had never been and never would be possible. She'd be an agent until she died.

With his thoughts returning to the darkness he wished to keep away, he stood from the table. He tossed his near-empty cup in the trash as he passed by the receptacle. Kieran marched directly to the elevator that would take him back to the suite. He had his own investigation to look into. He hoped that would keep his mind off everything else that was happening.

* * * *

Dakota's hand shook as she passed around copies of the report she'd typed up. It had taken hours, but she was happy with all the information she'd been able to gather. She'd drunk so much coffee that she was practically buzzing. Still, she'd managed to get through the morning without giving in to her exhaustion.

Not only were her two partners in the room, but so were Caspar, several of the agents in charge and three other agent teams. Even Damon and two of his Enforcers had arrived. She wished Kieran had been brought in, but he had his patrols and the threat of his father hanging over his head. Kieran had enough to deal with.

"As you can see, there have been two other instances where these rituals have taken place. In each case, the rituals started with animal sacrifices, moved to humans, then shifter. The humans were civilian, but the shifters killed were agents who worked for our Organization," she said. Dakota glanced at Damon. Caspar had agreed to bring the Alpha IN as long as Damon signed a non-disclosure contract. He wouldn't be able to talk about what he was hearing with anyone who wasn't currently in the room.

"At this time, we have no reason to believe that your Pack is in danger," she said. "But with the rituals taking place in your territory, I'm advising you to take precautions. They haven't used a shifter's territory before that we know of. They may target your Pack."

"Understood," Damon stated with a firm nod.

"If they continue to keep to their schedule, they might try for the next ritual tonight. I'd like to take you up on your offer to have our agents in the area," she said.

Damon pressed his lips together as he studied her. "If I allow your agents to trespass all over my territory, I insist that my Pack be involved."

Dakota looked over at Caspar. She couldn't give Damon the permission he requested, although having him and his Pack with her would make her feel a lot better.

"You are a civilian," Caspar pointed out. "If this group is linked to the other cases Dakota has found, we can't authorize putting you or your Pack in danger."

"I'll be involved whether you want me to be or not," Damon stated. "This is happening in my territory, as I've said before. Also, you're not some civilian agency that has a rule book that must be followed. We both know that you use civilians or anyone that falls within your paranormal parameter. I just happen to be volunteering."

Caspar didn't look to be swayed by Damon's statement.

"It is a big area, sir," Dakota said. "We could use all the help we can get. Plus Damon's Pack knows the area."

There were several long moments of tense silence until Caspar nodded. "They'll be your responsibility. Are you willing to take on so many untrained shifters into your op?"

Good question. Dakota was already dealing with a case that could blow up in her face. If they lost any innocent humans or agents because she missed something or didn't move fast enough, if would be her fault. So how would she feel if someone from Damon's Pack was injured or worse? Of course, if she didn't have Damon's help, it would be hard to end this investigation tonight. "I think I have to," she decided. Dakota looked at Caspar. "I think we need to do whatever we have to if we want to find these people before they begin to sacrifice humans."

Caspar nodded even though he looked as troubled as she felt. "Get your plan worked out for tonight." He looked over at Damon. "We appreciate your assistance."

Damon smirked. Everyone in the room knew that Caspar wasn't happy with Damon's involvement. That didn't matter to her, though. Dakota had to come up with a plan that would keep everyone safe.

Caspar stood. "Have your plan of action on my desk by thirteen hundred hours."

Shit, that only gave her about three hours. "Yes, sir."

Caspar left, with the other upper management agents with him. That just left Dakota, the agents who would back her up and Damon and his two shifters. Dakota rose and snatched one of the maps from the conference table. She unrolled it before motioning for Damon to join her.

"Can you mark the spots of the ritual spots you've already found?" she asked. Dakota handed him a red marker then picked up a green one. "Then we need to decide on which locations are the most likely to be used tonight. Green will be the highest possibility, orange the next, blue the next. And so on. We'll spread out as many teams as possible to cover what ground we can."

"If it makes you feel any better, I won't have untrained shifters running around. I have several military Pack members who will be perfect for this. They can blend into their environments and know the area well. I'm not sacrificing my Pack. I'm trying to protect them." Damon bent over the map as he spoke.

His words did make her feel better, but the worry that had been eating at her since she'd put together the information was still there. Twice the same rituals had led to humans being taken and killed. Twice they'd lost agents, first in Texas then outside of New York City. After sixteen rituals, the group had disappeared, without leaving much evidence behind. The first and second case had never been connected.

"Here, sir." Damon's guard—Seth, Dakota thought his name was—pointed to a section of the map. "I noticed the last time I was out that way there were more footprints than usual. It leads to a hard hiking trail. Not many people without experience could make it all the way. I've had bodybuilder types give up and turn around halfway."

"Good," Damon said. "That's good to know." He circled the area in green. "Anywhere else?"

"Let me make a few calls," Seth replied. "I'll find out. Rich and some of the other guys were going for a run this morning."

"Shit, I forgot about that," Damon said. "Call everyone back in. I don't want anyone running around on their own. We don't need to give them a target."

Dakota nodded. "I'm still waiting on some of the case files from the other two instances. I can't tell if they kidnapped the humans or agents in advance or took them straight to the ritual sites." She needed those damn files.

"Okay." Damon took a deep breath before meeting her gaze. "Let's talk this out."

Chapter Four

Kieran pulled his bike into the empty parking lot of an old dentist's office a block from the Organization. It was where he parked his bike instead of in the parking garage at the office. He wasn't really surprised to see a man leaning against the black SUV waiting on him in his secret parking place.

He turned off his motorcycle before swinging his leg over the bike. Kieran kept his backpack on as he looked the man up and down. Expensive light gray suit with shiny black shoes—Kieran really wanted to mess that outfit up. Maybe step on the tip of a shoe just to be a dick. He braced his feet before crossing his arms over his chest. "What are you doing here?"

James strode forward. "Just making sure you don't manage to ditch me again."

"Where's your partner?"

"Caden's meeting us at the office. I figured I could give you a ride."

Kieran had to give the human credit. He hadn't been scared off the night before and now here he was challenging Kieran. Okay, Kieran could play this game for a while. At least until he got bored. He strode forward. "I thought I told you to lose the suits." He yanked open the passenger door and put his backpack between his feet, making sure to keep it upright.

James climbed in behind the wheel. "And I told you that I look damn good in a suit."

He snorted. James was an attractive man in his early thirties. He was built and appeared to spend a lot of time working out. From the file he'd stolen, Kieran knew James was also smart. James had been the lead agent in Wyoming before he'd requested a transfer to Vegas. Kieran couldn't find in any paperwork why James had made that request. He'd have to keep an eye on the agent until Kieran figured out what had drawn James there. He'd been in town for three weeks and the timing was suspicious.

Kieran watched the other agent out of the corner of his eye. There was a good possibility that James was there to spy on Kieran for his father. Kieran wanted to think he was just paranoid, but he couldn't shake the feeling that there was more to James than what the agent was showing them.

Charlie was manning the gate once again and Kieran was saddened by the fact that he couldn't screw with the young guard. Charlie had become one of Kieran's favorite people at the office. He knew the guard was looking forward to more field time and Kieran was determined that he'd be a good agent. That he'd survive his time in the field.

"Good afternoon, Agent," Charlie greeted James. "Kieran?" Charlie bent down to peer at him. "Is everything okay?" He looked suspiciously at James.

Oh, this was perfect. He might not be able to screw with Charlie but James was fair game. "No, Charlie," Kieran replied calmly. "This man is a double agent who has kidnapped me to force me to let him into classified areas. He's holding a gun on me."

"For fuck's sake," James muttered.

Charlie had his weapon out of the holster and pressed against the side of James' head before Kieran could even blink. Kieran was going to have to make sure to tell Charlie how good he did. Later. After James got himself out of this clusterfuck.

"Put both hands on the wheel and keep them there," Charlie demanded.

James slowly followed the command. "Kieran."

"Don't say another word," Charlie ordered. His hand barely even shook as he held the weapon on James.

"Agent Grier, I have a six-four-four at the gate. I am requesting immediate assistance. Code red." Charlie spoke rapidly into the radio.

"Kieran," James growled.

"Don't move!" Charlie shouted at James even though James hadn't moved at all.

"I'm not moving. I did not kidnap Kieran," James tried to explain.

"He just jumped in your vehicle?" Charlie asked. "Next you'll tell me *he* kidnapped *you*."

"No," James replied. "I was giving him a ride from where he'd parked his bike."

"He couldn't walk a block?" Charlie asked. "Kieran never comes through the gate. Especially with an agent that isn't his partner or Dakota."

"Agent Grier, please contact the special agent in charge and Special Agent Dakota Reese." Charlie spoke into the radio again.

"This is fucking ridiculous," James snarled.

"I'm going to get out now," Kieran said. "Okay, Charlie? Keep an eye on him. I don't want to get shot in the back." Oh, he was going to hell for this stunt. But the look of rage on James' face was so perfect.

"I got your back, Kieran," Charlie said. "If he so much as twitches his pinkie, I'll blow his head off."

Kieran held back a chuckle. He was going to have to work with Charlie on his threats.

"Don't you dare leave me like this," James muttered.

Kieran winked at him. Then opened the passenger door and slid from the vehicle, only pausing long enough to grab his backpack.

The metal door to the stairwell burst open with agents in full riot gear swarming out. Kieran stepped away from the vehicle and laughed.

"Kieran!" James bellowed.

He cackled all the way past the SUV to lean against the building as the agents on site proceeded to drag James out of the vehicle and onto his stomach. A pity that the nice light gray suit was getting dirty as James struggled against getting cuffed.

"What did you do?" Remy asked as he relaxed next to Kieran.

"What do you mean?" Kieran questioned. "I just got here and saw all the commotion. Guess James did something to make Charlie suspicious."

Remy snorted, not believing a word.

"I'm going to fucking kill you, Kieran!" James yelled.

"Yeah." Remy gripped the back of Kieran's neck. "Let's get you out of here before Caspar arrives. I heard a rumor that your girl hasn't had a minute to rest and could use a break. No one's been able to get her to stop for a second. Maybe you'll have better luck. Everyone else left a couple of hours ago to prepare for the mission tonight."

Kieran didn't need to be told twice. He headed for the stairwell with Remy at his heels. "Where is she?"

"Main conference room."

He double-timed it, using his speed to reach the right floor in just a matter of minutes.

The door to the conference room was open. Kieran peered in, spotting Dakota leaning over a map of some sort. He walked into the room and closed the door behind him.

Dakota whirled around. "Kieran? What is this shit about you being held against your will by an agent?"

Fuck, she had dark circles under her eyes, her hair had come out of her bun and she appeared exhausted. "No idea what you're talking about. You must be more tired than you thought."

"Someone just radioed me—" She waved her hand. "Never mind, you're obviously fine."

"Obviously," he agreed. "Have you even slept?"

She shook her head. "I only had a couple of hours to put together the plan for tonight. Now I'm trying to figure out if I might have missed something."

Kieran stalked forward until he was pressing up against her. "You need rest so you're sharp tonight." If Dakota was running an op, Kieran needed to make sure that he was involved. He'd talk to Caspar but that could wait. Dakota needed him first. "Sit."

"I can't." She blinked up at him. "There's too much—"

Kieran yanked out a chair and shoved her down.

"Kieran," she said warily.

"I brought you something," he told her.

He placed his backpack down on the table before unzipping the top. Kieran pulled the plastic bag out and set it in front of her.

"Chinese?" she asked with need evident in her tone.

"Orange chicken, fried rice and egg rolls. Extra orange sauce," he responded.

"Oh, God," she exclaimed. Dakota pulled the bag toward her and ripped into it.

"And!" He produced a cold glass bottle of iced tea.

"Kieran." She rose then wrapped her arms around his neck. "Thank you."

He felt warm and pleasant, having made her so happy. There were so many times that he questioned what Dakota got out of a relationship with him. Kieran had so many quirks and such a horrid past that he would forever be broken. But the delight and love on her face at moments like these showed him that he was doing something right.

"Please eat," he whispered against her ear. "You can even fill me in as you have dinner. Something might pop as you talk it out."

"That's a good idea," she agreed. Dakota sat then patted the chair to her right. He sat close to her as she opened the plastic container and the aroma of orange sauce filled the room.

"Last I heard, you'd connected this investigation with two others," he said.

"Yes," she agreed. "I'm certain this group has been busy for decades. I don't think humans would be able to pull this off. The fact that they chose humans and shifters as their victims means that they have to be able to overpower their targets."

"Could still be humans," Kieran stated.

"Working for over forty years?" Dakota asked. "It's possible, but I just don't think so."

"You have good instincts. If you don't think so, I would have to agree."

"Thanks," she told him. "I've been racking my brain to try to figure out what the other agents missed and why they couldn't find this group before the disappeared."

"You'll figure it out."

Dakota shook her head. "I'm still waiting on the case files from New York. If I make a mistake, someone is going to die. A lot of someones by the end of this." She paused with her fork sitting in her container. "Now I have Damon's Pack involved and they aren't even trained agents."

"Hey." Kieran grasped her hands and brought them up to his lips. "It'll be okay."

"I hope so." She leaned her forehead against his. "I've never been in charge of such a large operation before. I'm terrified of screwing up."

Kieran made soothing noises as he comforted his lover. Now was the worst possible time for Dakota's niece to have shown up. He knew he couldn't tell Dakota about Kayla when she was already stressed out. He just hoped she wouldn't be too pissed at him when she found out he'd kept something so big from her.

"Got it!" Dare burst in the room.

"What?" Dakota lifted her head and Kieran barely managed to move out of the way before she clipped his chin.

"The final reports from New York are here. I noticed you hadn't opened the file yet so I printed it out for you," Dare said.

"Thanks." Dakota pulled back, out of Kieran's embrace, then grabbed the papers that Dare was waving around.

Kieran sighed, already missing the brief moment he'd had alone with Dakota.

The door opened again, but this time Caspar walked in with James trailing behind him. Oh shit, he'd forgotten that little episode.

"Agent Smith." Caspar only used his title when he was really pissed.

Dakota dropped the stack of papers on the table next to her half-eaten dinner. "What'd you do now?" she asked.

Kieran grinned. "Nothing." He rose. There was no way he'd let anyone stand over him. With the murderous glare that James was giving him, Kieran was in danger of being punched.

"Nothing?" James repeated quietly.

"Yeah, I bet." Dakota snorted.

"Kieran," Caspar said. "Can you explain why you told another agent that James here kidnapped you and was forcing you to get him into classified areas?"

"Classified areas?" Dakota asked. "We don't have classified areas here."

"I know!" Caspar roared.

Kieran sat back on the table top and swung his legs. "In my defense, it could have happened."

"No, it couldn't," Caspar stated.

"Maybe Charlie misread the situation," Kieran tried.

"Jeez." Dakota turned to him. "You involved Charlie? You know he's trying to get into the field."

"Good practice then," Kieran responded. "He handled himself very well. Stayed calm."

James stepped past Caspar. "Are you fucking kidding me?" he yelled. "I was dragged out of my car, forced on the ground and cuffed. If Caspar hadn't arrived when he did, I might be in holding right now."

"And you got your suit dirty," Kieran pointed out helpfully. "I told you that you shouldn't have worn it."

"Fucker!" James lunged for Kieran, but Caspar stepped between them.

Kieran hadn't even flinched. James might be a trained agent, but he was still human. Kieran wasn't worried that James would do any real damage. And even he could admit that James deserved to get at least one hit in.

"Calm down, James," Caspar told the other agent.

"I…" James was sputtering. Kieran really had to hold back his laugh. He was getting even more of a reaction than he'd expected.

"Kieran." Dakota nudged him. "Don't you think that was crossing a line?"

He peered at his lover as Dakota frowned at him. He grunted but hopped off the table. "Maybe I went a bit overboard this time."

Caspar growled. For a human, his boss sounded just like a shifter.

"Okay, okay." Kieran held his hands up. "I owe you an apology, James."

James crossed his arms over his chest. "What I can't figure out is why you did it. What did you get out of humiliating me in front of the entire office?"

Damn, this guy was taking the prank way too seriously.

"I didn't humiliate you," Kieran argued. "I was just welcoming you to the team."

"Welcoming me?" James asked.

"Sure, ask Remy how I introduced myself to him when we were first teamed together," Kieran said.

"No, don't," Caspar barked. "I don't need everyone knowing that we lost an agent for twenty-four hours."

Dakota laughed before slapping a hand over her mouth. Caspar glared at her since she wasn't hiding her mirth very well.

James gaped at Caspar. "Seriously?"

Caspar shook his head.

"I don't feel so bad now," James commented.

"You really shouldn't," Dakota said. "If he screws with you, it means he either likes you or he's warming up at least."

"*He* is standing right here," Kieran stated.

Caspar, James, Dakota and Dare all turned to look at him.

"What?" Kieran snapped. He just didn't like being ignored.

"He a good agent?" James asked as he eyed Kieran.

"Yes," Dakota answered.

"He is," Caspar said.

"As much as I hate to admit it," Dare said, "he really is the best."

James seemed to have to come to some sort of discussion. He held his hand out to Kieran. Kieran grinned before placing his palm against the other man's. James gripped him firmly then yanked him forward. "If you fuck me with me again, I'll kick your ass."

That was throwing a challenge that Kieran would find hard to ignore. Instead of speaking his thoughts, he simply nodded.

"Now that we've avoided that crisis, how about we get back to work?" Caspar suggested.

"I want to be involved in Dakota's op tonight," Kieran demanded.

Caspar curled his lips before he smiled. Kieran immediately grew concerned.

"Sure," Caspar told him. "You can team up with James for the night."

Kieran opened his mouth to argue with his boss, but Caspar held up his hand.

"If anything happens to James or you pull any pranks, I'll suspend you for two weeks. Two very long weeks where you can't come into the office or be involved in any cases we're currently investigating."

"That's low." Kieran pouted.

"I mean it, Kieran," Caspar said.

"Fine," Kieran agreed. "I won't play with the new agent."

Caspar didn't look amused as he left the room.

* * * *

Dakota had handed out assigned areas to the agents and Damon's people. The group had separated to get started on the rounds. Kieran stood with Damon and James, watching as she tried to make last-minute changes, again. Kieran had seen enough.

"Come here." Kieran drew her away from the map she'd spread out of the hood of her SUV.

"I have to—" She waved her marker around.

"You have to take a breath," he said. "We've gone through tonight every which way possible. If anything happens, you did everything in your power to stop it."

"Not going to matter if they kill someone tonight," she muttered.

Kieran didn't know what was wrong with her. She was never this indecisive. She had been running ops for years now and had led teams into firefights where the threat of death was high. "It's been a hard couple of days and you've taken on too much. You're worried about me, our friends and now this investigation." Kieran wasn't used to being the voice of reason. He sort of liked this change in their relationship, or he would, if he knew what to say. He glanced over at Damon and James for help, but the two men were too busy glaring at each other to offer him any assistance.

The moment Kieran had pulled up, James had asked about the tall, handsome Alpha. After Kieran had explained to James that Damon was the Alpha wolf shifter leader of the local Pack who had helped them previously in several cases, James had wanted to meet him.

Only minutes later, the two men had begun sniping at each other.

Kieran was pretty sure that he'd missed something, but he didn't want to ask. Remy had seemed amused, so Kieran figured it was a shifter thing.

"I guess you're right," she conceded. "It's too late to do anything about it now."

"That's the spirit." Kieran kissed her briefly before gesturing to her map. "Now let's get to work."

"Okay." Dakota strode back over to her map then started folding it back up. She slipped it into her pocket before gesturing to Damon. "You ready?"

Damon tore his gaze away from James and nodded. "It'll be easier if we shift and run from here."

"And leave the non-shifters behind," James muttered.

Kieran stepped up to James' side. Remy had been teamed up with Caden so Kieran was stuck with the human. "It'll be fine. We don't need to shift in order to do our job."

"Maybe you should go back to the office," Damon said to James. "Wouldn't want you to get hurt playing with the big boys."

James fisted his hands as he took a step forward.

"Damn it." Dakota grabbed Damon's arm. "You two can fuck later. We have work to do."

"What?" Kieran squeaked. "They're fucking?"

"Not yet," Dakota told him. "But they want to."

Damon snorted. "I'm not sure he'd have time in his busy schedule."

"Fuck you," James spat.

"Maybe if you're a good boy." Damon ran his gaze up and down James' body.

Kieran knew that James was going to try to hit Damon even before James moved. Using his superior speed, he caught James in a bear hug and carried him away.

Behind him, Dakota was laying into Damon for provoking James.

"Put me down," James demanded.

Kieran dropped him back onto his feet but kept his hand on the human's shoulder. He guided James to their vehicle. "I'm not sure what that was about, but now's not the time."

"Sorry," James said. "Fuck, that was unprofessional."

It wasn't like Kieran had any room to judge—he was the most unprofessional agent in the office.

He waited until James had climbed into the passenger seat before he got behind the wheel.

"Want to talk about it?" Kieran finally asked. Okay, his curiosity was killing him. He really hoped James did.

"We met last weekend at one of the bars off the Strip," James said. "I flirted with him, but he was with a bunch of other people and didn't want to go into the back room. I ended up hooking up with another guy."

"Oh." Kieran hadn't even known the Alpha was gay. Not that he cared, but he felt as though he should know the Alpha better since Dakota had sort of implied he was part of their tight circle.

"I asked around about him and found out that he's bi, not gay," James supplied. "In case you were wondering."

Kieran shrugged a shoulder. "I just never thought about it, I guess. Now I feel bad for not knowing him better."

"From what the bartender told me, Damon doesn't get out a lot and when he does, he usually goes home alone. Hasn't been in a serious relationship for several years."

"You found all that out in one night?" Kieran asked. It sounded like James had been more than casually interested in the Alpha.

"The bartender is who I ended up going home with," James said. "We had to talk about something in between fucking."

Kieran laughed. "But you talked about another guy?"

"Well yeah," James replied with a smirk. "I'd been trying to get Damon's attention all evening and Kyle, the bartender, had also been trying, for months. It came up."

"Okay," Kieran said. "What happened tonight?"

James clenched his jaw then turned to stare out of the window.

"James?"

"I guess he smelt the guy I was with before my shift. He said some unflattering things," James confided.

"Did he call you a slut?" Kieran asked. "Because if he tried to slut shame you, I'll kick his ass."

"*Slut shame?*" James repeated.

"I have internet," Kieran told him. "I know things."

James started to laugh, hard, so hard he eventually had to wipe the tears from his eyes. "Holy shit, dude!" he gasped.

"What?" Kieran wasn't even trying to be funny.

"Sorry! Sorry!" James waved his hands in front of him. "That's got to be the best thing that anyone has ever said to me."

Kieran grumbled.

"It was also a very nice thing to offer," James said. "Thanks."

"I meant it." Kieran had. He might not know what he thought about the other agent yet, but no one should be made to feel bad about what or who they did in the bedroom. He and Dakota could get a little rough and had their kinks.

"It's fine," James told him. "He wasn't completely off base. Do you know why I asked for the transfer here?"

"No," Kieran confessed. "It wasn't in your file."

"It wouldn't be. My old supervisor was a homophobe. I wasn't allowed to mention one thing about my sexual preference. If he thought I was about to 'act gay' I'd get sent to extra training sessions."

Kieran tightened his grip on the wheel. "Does Caspar know?"

"He does now. He drilled me about why I asked for the transfer until I confessed what was happening. My old supervisor has been demoted and an investigation is open."

"Good." Kieran hated any kind of prejudice. Life was hard enough without people acting like such assholes. Who the fuck cared what people did in their own time as long as no one was getting hurt? In his opinion, people just needed to mind their own fucking business and the world would be a much more peaceful place.

"But my point is that I couldn't go out and meet people because I was afraid my boss would find out. I was only with other men twice a year when I went on vacation. And forget about finding a partner to build a life with. Wasn't possible."

"Then you got here and went crazy with the freedom," Kieran guessed.

"Exactly," James said. "I hadn't meant to. I really do want to find someone who wants to be with me for more than one night."

"You're not going to find that person at a bar," Kieran said.

"Really?" James sounded amused. "Where'd you meet Dakota?"

Oh shit. The first night he'd met Dakota, she'd followed him into the bar of the casino they were currently living in. But he'd seen her before that. "A dark alley."

"What?" James barked.

"I was supposed to be on vacation," Kieran said. "Caspar sent me here. Now I know he had his reasons, but, at the time, I thought he was trying to plant me somewhere out of his way."

"What did you do?" James asked, sounding very much like all the other people in his life. As if he knew Kieran had done something.

"I was bored," he defended.

"Uh-huh."

"I might have also been looking for trouble," he conceded. "I came across some asshole shifters messing with some humans. I stopped them. I had to call into the office here since technically I had no jurisdiction or place to put them. Since I was on vacation and all that."

"I can just imagine how much Dakota loved some stranger coming into her city and making trouble."

"I was taking care of trouble," Kieran corrected. Although, in truth, James was right. If it'd been anyone other than Kieran, the agent would have been in trouble. "Dakota was the agent called out."

"Was it love at first sight?" James teased.

Kieran laughed. "She hated me on sight. Although it turns out she'd been assigned to follow me to make sure I stayed out of trouble. So her opinion was biased."

"What about you?"

"I was….confused," he finally settled on. "She was a shifter, but I was instantly drawn to her. It gave me a few rough moments." Admittedly, some of those moments had been his worst. That first meeting with Dakota had been the start of his life unraveling. Although Kieran was happy, he wasn't big on change and it had seemed to him that his world had been turned on its head.

"That sounds about right," James commented.

"But Dakota knew what she wanted and wouldn't let my prejudices get in the way."

"She fought for you. Even against you."

"We're meant to be," he stated proudly. "I believe that now."

James hummed as he sat back in his seat while Kieran continued the drive to their designated area. Kieran left the human to his own thoughts. It was James' life, but now that Kieran knew his story, he'd like to see James find what he'd come searching for.

* * * *

"Do you want to talk about it?" Dakota asked Damon. The Alpha was glaring at the SUV as Kieran drove off.

She'd picked up the interest between Damon and James right away. The scent of arousal and interest had flooded the space between the two men. Then Damon had shut the feelings down so fast that it had practically left her reeling. She didn't know how to help the Alpha.

"Doesn't matter," Damon muttered. "You ready to shift?"

"Sure," she agreed. Dakota knew better than to push Damon. The Alpha was so much like Kieran that she would have been amused if she hadn't had so many other things on her mind.

Damon stalked off. Dakota turned then strode to the back of her own vehicle. She and Damon were going to wander around on all fours and try to pick up any scents that didn't belong in the area.

She opened the hatch to the back before undressing.

The cool wind of the evening caressed her flesh as she bared her naked body to the environment. As a shifter, she had no trouble removing her clothes around others as was normal before transforming. Still, she appreciated Damon giving her privacy. Once she'd tossed the clothes inside her vehicle, she closed the hatch then dropped down onto the dusty ground.

Dakota closed her eyes as she pictured her jaguar form.

Her body shuddered as she changed into the large feline. Fur replaced skin, her hands turned to paws and in a moment she went from human to animal.

There was no pain, just the relief of releasing her jaguar.

It really had been too long since she'd shifted.

A long howl drew her attention to the other shifter close by. Even though she kept full control of her mind and thought with human intelligence, her jaguar instincts were strong. She knew it was just Damon celebrating his transformation, but the feline part of her wanted to pounce.

With caution, she crept around the side of the SUV before dropping down next to the tire.

The Alpha wolf had his head bent back toward the moon as she spied on him. Then Damon peered right at her.

Dakota watched him for any sense of danger. She was a powerful feline and could hold her own against most other shifters. However, even from several yards away, she could literally feel the power coming off the Alpha. He might be—probably was—the strongest shifter in the city.

The sound that Damon made soothed and comforted her. She crawled forward, slowly, until he lowered himself to show he wasn't a threat. Even though she wasn't part of his Pack, she still wanted his approval. *The weaker animal seeking the strength of the true Alpha.* She felt the same way about Kieran and he wasn't even a shifter. But the absolute power that Kieran sent out had her wanting to roll over and bare her vulnerable stomach to her lover.

Damon nuzzled her neck as she reached him. The motion was not sexually but instead done in a fatherly fashion. Dakota might not have experience with a parental figure, but she craved the contact.

She pawed at Damon's leg before she dropped down, pressing her weight against him. Damon didn't budge but continued to mark him with the scent of Alpha and Pack. Once he seemed satisfied, he rolled her onto her feet. Dakota stretched her long body out then licked her lips.

She was ready to hunt.

Her prey wouldn't know what had come for them until it was too late.

Damon growled before he took off at a fast run. She easily caught up with him and they ran side by side. He knew the area better than her, so she allowed him to take the lead even though this was her mission. Dakota knew to use the assets she had available to her and Damon being on their team would make a huge difference.

Out in the Red Rocks, there were no lights, just natural moonlight guiding their paths. The humans would need flashlights or lanterns, so that would help spot them.

She knew the hours were passing as she and Damon circled, climbed and ran through their assigned positions over and over. Each time they didn't find anyone, she grew more and more frustrated.

Damon wasn't faring much better. He'd slowed their pace while continuing to lift his muzzle to the air, trying to scent around them. Dakota trotted away, giving Damon the space to get a clear reading of aromas. She doubted they'd find anything tonight. There'd been no word from the other teams, which didn't bode well for the entire mission.

She'd run the numbers for hours and everything she'd gotten from the files had told her that the next ritual should take place tonight. What had she missed? Dakota tried to rerun the information she'd read but couldn't figure out where she'd gone wrong. The sadistic group that had obviously been in the area before should still be here.

Behind her Damon howled. As she turned, he flew by her.

Dakota scrambled to catch up.

The Alpha was tearing over the vast land at an unbelievable speed. This proved to her that Damon had been holding back for her earlier. Panting, she raced to keep him in sight. She had no idea what they were heading into.

Ahead of her, Damon slowed to a stop. She was still trying to catch her breath as she reached his side. He nudged her to the north and Dakota could smell them. Humans, male and female, had walked through mere moments ago. Holy shit, were they actually going to catch these assholes?

Not far from where they stood was a break in the rocks. Dakota nosed Damon's shoulder, nodding to where they could hide. Maybe the group did their rituals closer to sunrise than she'd counted on? Dakota had figured the sacrifices were taking place between midnight and three in the morning. But since the sun would be coming up within the hour, she'd guessed wrong. Luckily, Damon had picked up the humans coming into the area. They'd almost missed them.

Dakota pressed herself into the tiny space allowed within the cave before Damon practically crawled on top of her. It wasn't comfortable, but she didn't want to scare off the other members of the group if they were arriving as well. She wished for a phone to call in back-up but quickly decided that she couldn't chance going back to the vehicle.

Kieran had a knack for showing up when she got into trouble, so Dakota hoped he'd come through once again.

She tried to listen for more activity in the area, but she didn't hear anything in the quiet of the too-early morning.

Damon had his head cocked toward the opening in the cave then shook his head.

Dakota squirmed out from under him and into the open of the cave.

She called forward her human form and waited until Damon did the same. "Just the two?" she whispered.

He nodded.

"Shit."

"I don't smell blood or anything matching the scents from the other sites," he told her.

"We need to get closer," she decided.

"I believe so."

Ignoring the fact that they were both naked in the middle of the desert, Dakota carefully made her way in the direction the humans had gone. Unlike the humans, Dakota and Damon didn't make any sounds as they walked. Following at a discreet distance, Dakota gave the humans space and time. As much as she wanted to pounce and tear out the humans' throats, she needed to catch them in the act, to at least setting up for a ritual. Dakota wouldn't allow another animal – or God forbid human – to get sacrificed.

"I'm not certain these are the ones we're after," Damon whispered.

Dakota wanted to disagree but remained silent. Until she knew for sure, these were the best suspects she had. She paused at the base of a tall, skinny tree. The sky was starting to lighten, but she was still hidden in the shadows.

The two humans slipped through a crack between two cave walls. It would be a perfect place for a ritual.

She waited for a few long moments then jerked back.

"Yeah," Damon said with a chuckle. "Pretty damn sure these humans aren't going to be sacrificing anyone."

"We don't know that," Dakota replied lamely. She really needed to close this case so she could concentrate to watching out for Kieran and his father.

There was a soft moan from the cave and Dakota slumped back against the tree. The two humans could be having sex before they set up for the ritual, but with the early morning hour she knew that they hadn't come across the sickos she was hunting. She didn't know where to go from here. Damn it, they'd have to do this all over again that night.

"Are we going to stay here and wait until they finish?" Damon questioned.

"No, let's go." She gave in.

Damon grinned before gesturing her forward.

She stomped off with the Alpha at her back. She waited until she would be hidden if the humans came out of the cave then shifted into her jaguar.

They weaved their way back and forth through the trails until they got back to her vehicle. Dakota was only half-surprised that Kieran was waiting leaning against the hood of the SUV. Usually he couldn't stay out of her business.

"I heard you coming back," he told her. "I decided to wait here for you instead of tracking you down." He slid his gaze to Damon. "Even with the Alpha with you." Kieran patted her head before strolling to the back of the vehicle. He opened the back hatch then pulled out her clothes.

Dakota watched him with amusement.

Kieran didn't want her shifting and staying naked. For a paranormal being, he had a strange aversion to her being naked. Well, naked with anyone but him.

Even though she would never admit it, Dakota loved Kieran's possessiveness.

He crouched down in front of her. "Are you going to shift back?"

She cocked her head, more interested in playing than going back to work.

"No," he told her. "We need to get back to the hotel. We didn't find anything, so we'll have to do this again." Kieran frowned. "Although maybe this time, we can send the Alpha with someone else."

Dakota took that moment to transform back.

Kieran caught her in his arms as she wavered. Shifting so many times wore her out. "Here." He pulled an energy bar from his pocket. "Eat this."

"Thanks." She ripped the wrapper off and shoved half of the bar in her mouth. Once she'd finished it off, Kieran helped her stand. Her legs still felt like Jell-O, but she was steady enough to at least get home.

"Get dressed so we can get out of here," he ordered.

It was on the tip of her tongue to argue, but Kieran lifted his hand to caress her cheek. "It's been a long night worrying about you. I just want to lie in bed with you for a few hours."

She never got tired of Kieran's softer side. "Yes, let's get home."

Chapter Five

The buzzing from the nightstand table wouldn't stop, no matter how long Dakota tried to ignore the annoying sound.

"I'm going to throw that fucking device out of the window," Kieran muttered.

She moaned and rubbed her face against the pillow. Dakota didn't want to get up. It couldn't have been more than two hours since she and Kieran had finally made it to bed. She was tired.

"Dakota!" he complained.

"Fine." She threw out an arm, knocking things off the table, until she reached her cell. Dakota held the stupid phone up and saw the string of text messages. "Fuck."

"What?" Kieran still sounded groggy.

"There's been another ritual, a murder—human victim."

"No!" Kieran sat up then flipped the switch on the lamp. "That's impossible. We had every inch of the rocks covered."

"Yeah, well." Dakota paused to respond to the text from Dare. Then she dropped her phone into her lap and turned to face Kieran. "The scene is only a block from here. In an old apartment complex."

"What the fuck?" Kieran growled out. "That doesn't make sense. Why would they move to the city? It's much more dangerous."

Dakota agreed. Why would this group switch sites? They hadn't done that in the past. Not even when the police had been close. "They knew we were out there."

"How?" Kieran demanded. He was already up and pulling on a black pair of pants, his tight utilities with dozens of pockets. He was going out in full badass mode. Kieran was pissed.

Well, so was she.

Dakota threw the covers off and rose. She stretched her back out, much like she would as a cat, then went into the bathroom. As she cleaned up and pulled her hair into a ponytail, she tried to put together her next plan of action.

Had there been a leak of some kind? Could someone on her team have betrayed them? Why else would the new scene be inside the city? And so close to her home? That couldn't be a coincidence. Dakota had a bad feeling in the pit of her stomach.

"If you scrub your teeth any harder, you'll break the brush."

Dakota jerked, focusing on what she was doing. Kieran stood in the doorway of the bathroom, peering at her. She recognized the concern in his eyes. Dakota finished rinsing out her mouth then put the toothbrush back. "I'm fine," she said, as she strolled past him.

"There's nothing you could have done," Kieran said.

She snorted as she walked to the closet. Obviously, Dakota should have done a better job. If she'd found whatever piece she was missing, someone wouldn't be dead.

"Dakota."

"I heard you," she said. Dakota didn't want to talk to her lover right then. She needed to think. They'd known the group would move on to humans, but she'd thought she'd have more time.

He sighed but didn't press her anymore.

Within fifteen minutes of getting the text message, she and Kieran were out of the door of their suite. Inside the elevator, Dakota tried to center herself. The anger and fury that was bubbling up wouldn't help. She needed to be able to focus.

The *ding* of arriving downstairs jolted her.

Kieran grabbed her arm before she could exit. "What can I do?"

Dakota shook her head. He was a good man and didn't deserve her anger directed at him. "Just help me," she told him. "I need you to find what we missed."

"I don't think we missed anything. I read through your case notes and we did what we could. You haven't had the files even twenty-four hours yet."

"I know." She caught the door when it would have closed. "But that doesn't help whoever was killed last night when we were in the desert."

"We'll catch these assholes," Kieran stated.

"Yes, we will," she vowed. "But how many more people will die?"

He let go of her arm and she walked out and to the back door. "If we cut through the parking lot, we'll be at the apartment building." Dakota pointed to the flashing lights of the patrol cars. "Shit, we can see the door from here."

"It's a message," Kieran spat. "The fuckers know we're working the case. They could have seen when we got in this morning."

Holy shit. Dakota's jaguar wanted out to hunt and kill. She actually became dizzy with the need to shift. Kieran squeezed her elbow as he shook.

"Deep breath," Kieran murmured. "That's it. Breathe again. There are humans all around us."

"I want to hurt them," she confessed.

"I know." He kissed the back of her head. "You in control now?"

"Yeah, Thanks."

"Come on then," Kieran said. "I see Remy. What's he doing here?"

That was a good question. Technically Kieran and Remy weren't on this case except to help with searches.

Remy met them halfway across the parking lot. His hands shook as he rubbed them over his mouth.

"You okay?" she asked.

"It's bad," Remy said. "Real fucking bad. I've seen some fucked-up shit, but this…damn."

"What are you doing here anyway?" Kieran asked.

"Caspar called all of us in. We're to help Dakota any way we can."

She nodded. She'd take it. "Thanks. What can you tell me?"

"A young man was sacrificed sometime last night or early this morning," Remy said. "The scene looks like the ritual sites, same markings."

"Shit, okay. I guess I need to see it."

Remy hung back as she and Kieran climbed the steps of the taped-off unit. She knew it was going to be just as bad as Remy had said when the young patrol officer outside the door was actually green.

Dakota didn't say anything as she ducked under the tape.

If she hadn't already studied the photos in the previous investigations, Dakota would have likely vomited on the crime scene. As it was, she clamped a hand over her mouth and nose as she peered around.

There was blood, so much blood, and it was everywhere. The floor, walls, ceiling. She couldn't pick up any scents other than blood.

The carpet had been torn out at some point so bare concrete showed the gleam of blood and body fluids. Dakota didn't know if the killers had stripped the room or if it had already been like this.

"We'll need to talk to the management of the complex," she said.

"I'll have Remy get their information," Kieran said.

As sick as she felt, she had to view the scene with the eyes of an investigator and not think about the horror the young man had gone through.

She knelt down beside the nude body.

The poor kid couldn't have been older than twenty-five or so.

His throat had been slit and marks cut into every inch of his flesh. The lack of bruising and other injuries was consistent with the victims from the other cases. The symbol that had connected her case to the other two was right over where his heart was. He'd suffered terribly.

"Who are you?" she asked the deceased young man. "How'd they pick you?" Dakota knew there wouldn't be answers, but she didn't normally have work homicides. The Organization was there to stop anyone from the paranormal community from committing crimes. This wasn't what she'd been trained to do, but Dakota wasn't giving up this case.

"Dakota."

She peered over her shoulder as Caspar stepped into the room, with Kieran behind him. Her boss flinched as he took in the scene.

"Jesus," Caspar whispered.

"I'm not letting the locals take this case," she said as she stood. "I'm getting these bastards."

Caspar nodded. "I have the pull to make that happen. We know from your research that there's been two other cases." He continued to look around. "Be sure, though. This is a lot to deal with."

Dakota dropped her gaze to the poor young man who'd lost his life in the most brutal fashion. "I'm sure."

Caspar nodded. "Dean is here. He is going to run the forensics for this. He's lead tech, so make sure everything is run by him."

She hadn't gotten to work with her old partner since he'd moved to the lab after they'd met Kieran. "Okay. Warn him before he comes up here." Dean hadn't liked the field much. He much preferred being in his lab, looking through a microscope.

"I will. The city coroner will take custody of the body," Caspar said. "There's nothing I can do about that, but he'll work with us. He has before."

Dakota started to argue but stopped when a tall, slim man stepped up to the doorway. She immediately scented the shifter. Dakota narrowed her eyes as he entered the apartment. Bird of some kind, and her jaguar did not like him.

"Dr. Bryce Gilmore," he announced when he'd taken a few steps forward. "I take it we won't have a problem here?"

She knew he was asking about her feline. Dakota was a professional, though, and simply nodded. The doctor still remained wary of her as he made a circle and approached the body from the other side.

"Poor bastard," Dr. Gilmore murmured.

Dakota crouched. "Can you tell me anything? Anything that might help?"

"He was alive when the cuts were carved into his skin. He would have fought — you can see the abrasions on his wrists and ankles as he struggled. I'm surprised no one heard him."

That would need to be looked into. Even if they'd tried to muffle him, someone should have heard something. Mentally, she began a list of everything that needed to be done. Caspar wanted to give her back up with all the teams available, but she didn't actually think that was a good idea. Someone had to have told the killers not to go into the desert.

"Anything else?" she asked.

"Not right now. I need to get him back to the office. I'll try to ID him for you."

"I might be able to help with that," Dean stated from behind her. He wasn't looking at the body but around the room. "My team can come in?" he asked her.

Dakota nodded. "Whenever you want."

"Let me get the body removed first," Dr. Gilmore said. "Then we'll be out of your way."

"Dean, you're in charge of this scene. Don't release it after you're done. I want someone on the door at all times," she ordered. Dakota turned to the coroner. "I'll check back with you later, but if you come across anything that might help, please give me a call." She passed him a card.

"Yes, Agent." Dr. Gilmore actually smiled at her with amusement. She didn't know why and it made her suspicious. She'd have the doctor watched, closely. Gilmore turned to her former partner. "Dean, it's good to see you again."

Wait, they knew each other?

As her ex-partner began to converse with the doctor, Dakota stepped back, watching. After a few boring minutes in which they spoke about a conference they'd attended, she let her gaze wander.

The apartment was small. A living room slash bedroom and a bath and kitchen. The entire space couldn't be much bigger than three hundred feet or so. It was such a small area but had served the purpose well enough, she supposed.

How had they known it was an empty apartment, though?

She strolled to the open door and stared across the long parking lot to the back door of her hotel. The home she'd made with Kieran.

Kieran was right.

The group was taunting them. They had known that the investigators would be out of the city. Which led her to think about who could have betrayed him. The problem was she knew the agents she worked with, except for James and Caden. But they were both just like them. To go against the Organization was almost unheard of.

The Organization wasn't like normal human police agencies. There was no recruitment or change of minds later. With the Organization being a birthright, the members served until they were too old to be an agent, or died. To betray the Organization wasn't something easily done.

Would either James or Caden risk their lives for this group?

Almost immediately, she discounted Caden being involved. He was a lion shifter. This group had killed shifters before so him being involved just didn't make sense. That left her with James. The human agent. He'd been in Wyoming before transferring to the Vegas office. She needed to get her hands on his personal file.

Dakota drifted to the edge of the balcony. Below her, there were human officers, agents from the Organization and her team milling around. It didn't seem that anyone was certain about what they should be doing. Caspar passed next to a black SUV while speaking on the phone. Farther away behind the black and yellow police tape, a gathering of spectators were craning to see what was going on.

One young woman, a teenage girl, caught Dakota's attention since she was staring right at Dakota.

Dakota narrowed her eyes to take in the young woman. And young she was. Her long hair was pulled back just like Dakota wore hers. The girl, dressed in jeans and a hoodie, didn't stop staring even when it was obvious Dakota was watching her. Instead she grinned before turning into the crowd.

"Hey!" Dakota yelled. She raced down the steps.

Kieran, Remy and James met her at the bottom of the steps.

"What is it?"

"Young girl, jeans with a hole in the right knee, with a black solid hoodie. Five foot two, brown hair pulled back and black shoes. Find her," Dakota called out as she continued toward the crowd.

The onlookers didn't move back as the agents swarmed. Dakota shoved people, but she'd lost sight of the girl.

Fuck, Dakota couldn't see the girl anywhere. She finally made it through the crowd and to the end of the apartment complex. She looked down an alley but didn't see anyone. *Shit.*

Catching her breath, she tried to pick up a scent. There were just too many strangers in the area. Plus she could still smell the blood from the small apartment.

"God damn it!" she yelled.

"I didn't see anyone." Kieran jogged over. Further south, James was looking in Dumpsters as he checked another alley. Remy was already heading back to them. They'd lost her.

"She was there," Dakota said. "She fucking smiled at me."

"That's pretty ballsy," Remy commented.

"So was slaughtering someone within view of the home of the agents hunting them," Dakota responded.

James started back in their direction and Dakota didn't want to say much in front of him.

"I want to talk to the manager of the complex," she said. "Kieran, can you get us set up in the suite? I want to come back over after the coroner leaves and Dean is done. Then after dark, to shift."

"Sure," Kieran replied. The way he was watching her, Dakota knew he was picking up on the fact that something was wrong.

"Remy, can you stay with the coroner?" she asked. "I don't trust him."

"He's a shifter," Remy told her.

Dakota nodded. "That doesn't mean anything to me right now. Someone knew we would be gone and where Kieran and I live. I trust no one we don't know well."

Kieran glanced over his shoulder where James was approaching. He was human so he wouldn't be able to overhear them. "And James?"

"I'll put him with Dean. With the way Dean and his team triple-check everything, it will keep him out of our hair for a while," she confessed.

"You think he might be involved?" Kieran sounded surprised.

"I don't know him or his partner. But I do know the other agents who were there last night."

"The wolf Pack was there too," Kieran pointed out.

Remy snorted. "Come on, K."

Kieran shrugged. "I'm just saying."

"He's right," Dakota interrupted Remy. "Damon's not involved, but we know this group has been around for a long time. We do have to consider that someone paranormal is involved."

"I run with them," Remy reminded her.

"I know. That's why I'm putting Dare and Gabe on the Pack to ask questions. They found the first sites, they know the area better than anyone else and knew where we'd be. Damon will not be happy, but his Pack needs to be questioned. They can take Caden with them. Two shifters will have a better chance of spotting someone lying or nervous."

"Damon's going to be pissed," Remy said.

"I don't have time to worry about that right now," she responded. This was going to hurt her relationship with the Alpha, but the image of the young man upstairs was burned into her brain. She was going to stop anyone else from being killed.

"Okay," Remy shuffled his feet. "I guess I can understand."

"Hey." James joined them. "I didn't see any sign of anyone."

Dakota nodded. The human agent seemed sincere, but that didn't mean much. He was a trained agent. She waved over Dare, Gabe and some of the other agents to pass out assignments. It was time to get to work.

She watched her team walk away but caught Kieran's sleeve before he could head out. "Can you get a hold of Mitch and ask him to meet me in our suite in an hour?"

"Mitch?" Kieran asked.

"Please. I'll explain when I get back."

Kieran nodded slowly. "Okay."

"Thanks." She wanted to kiss him, but there were too many damn witnesses. She peered around one more time, hoping to catch sight of the young girl, but wasn't lucky enough. Instead she turned on her heel and headed toward the apartment leasing office.

* * * *

Kieran was worried about his lover.

The scene had been horrible and she was taking the murder hard. There was no way that any of them could have known what was going to happen, but Dakota wouldn't see it that way.

All he could do was support her until they tracked down the killers. And they would find out who was responsible. Kieran was the best tracker in the world. He'd been able to pick up a few clues that might help. There had been five others in the room with the murder victim. It'd been hard to pick up the induvial scents, but he could separate them enough to figure out that much.

Kieran used the same elevator he'd earlier been in with Dakota and thought about how many things she had on her plate right then. He still hadn't found the time to tell her about her niece and knew he needed to. Hopefully the young girl would give him time before she introduced herself to her aunt. Kieran did not see that meeting going well if Dakota was surprised.

Plus, there had still been no word from his father.

Kieran wanted to go to Texas himself to see what was happening at his family's compound, but he couldn't leave in the middle of an investigation of this caliber.

Once inside his suite, he went straight to the closet in the living room. With two agents living there, they'd worked from the suite plenty of times. He pulled out the cork board and slid it in front of the television. He did the same with the white erase board. The files were still in Dakota's bag, so he began to post them up. He used a piece of tape to divide the board into thirds – the two previous cases and the current one.

He knew Dakota, so it was easy to prepare her display. Once happy he'd done what he could, he pulled out his phone and texted Mitch. The young IT expert had become a good friend of theirs and responded right away he'd be there soon. Kieran went into the kitchen and started a pot of coffee and made sure they had cold water in the fridge. There were benefits to living in a full-service hotel but he could at least make coffee.

Once the coffee was brewing, he returned to the living room and picked up a red marker. On the far right side of the white erase board, he started to list what they knew about the case. At the bottom he wrote, *5 suspects*.

By the time he'd finished writing, the door to the suite opened and Dakota walked in. She looked exhausted and let the door close loudly behind her.

"Come here," he urged.

She stood in place and just shook her head.

Kieran went to his lover and yanked her into his arms. She buried her face against his chest and wept. He didn't know what to do so he held her tight and rocked her. After she stopped shuddering, he leaned back and cupped her chin.

"He was so young," Dakota said. "Why would someone do that to him?"

"I don't know," Kieran confessed.

"I spoke to Dean again before I left. He thinks they had him for hours before they finally slit his throat. He would have suffered horribly."

"We'll stop them," Kieran said.

She nodded. "Before they do this again?"

"If we can," he said truthfully. "We know that they've done this before and they're masters."

"Is it humans that are doing this? If they kill shifters, surely shifters aren't involved."

"Walkers," Kieran said.

Dakota shook her head. "Walkers are solitary. They stay with their families and don't work like this. Why would they need the rituals, anyway? A Walker can kill anyone they want anytime."

"Then who?" Kieran questioned.

"I don't know," she replied. "What about James? Can we really trust him?"

Kieran had a feeling that was where his lover's thoughts had gone. It had been obvious to him at the scene that the human had caught her attention. "Sit. I'll get you some coffee and you can explain it to me." He didn't believe James had betrayed them. Not after spending time with the man the previous night.

"I'm gonna go to the bathroom. Give me a few minutes, then I'll lay it out for you."

He let her go then made his way to the kitchen. He poured two cups of coffee and carried them into the living room. He set them both on the coffee table before glancing at the window. The curtains were still drawn, so he walked over and pulled them open. From their window, the edge of the crime scene was visible. He could see the actual apartment, but the police tape was still holding back the crowd that had grown.

"See anything?" Dakota asked as she joined him.

"No, I can't see the apartment, but there's a pretty good crowd still out there."

"Is the coroner's van still there?"

"He just pulled away," Kieran told her.

"Good. I want to get an ID quickly. That young man has family somewhere who will be missing him."

"Either Dean or Dr. Gilmore will figure it out." He turned as she picked up her mug.

"Wait — you know the coroner too?"

"I know of him," Kieran responded. "Caspar trusts him. He works closely with us or has in the past."

"He smiled at me."

"When?" Kieran questioned.

"Inside the apartment, when we were talking. He was amused."

"I can imagine," Kieran said.

"What? Why?"

"You realize you actually licked your lips when he walked in, right? You were sizing him up."

"I was not!"

"Babe, your jaguar was so close to the surface that your eyes had turned gold. I was worried you would shift inside the apartment."

Dakota frowned at him. "I wasn't going to shift." She pouted at him, looking utterly adorable. "And don't call me babe."

He knew the pet name would irritate her. Kieran chuckled. "Yes, dear."

She narrowed her eyes but also grinned. There, that was better. Kieran picked up his coffee and joined her on the couch.

"Did you get anything from the manager of the apartments?"

"No manager," she said. "The apartments are empty. The complex just sold, and no one's around to hear what was happening."

"Fuck," he spat. Just their luck.

"That information couldn't be common knowledge."

"I'll ask Jackson or Alex. They know everything that's going on around the casino."

"Good idea," she praised.

"Tell me why you suspect James, because after working with him, I don't see it."

"He's human," she said.

Kieran lifted an eyebrow. Dakota wasn't the type of agent who was prejudiced toward humans. Dean and she had been partners for a decade and still remained close. Dakota was often a champion for the human agents, making sure the paranormal agents didn't mistreat them.

"There were only two agents who I didn't know personally that had inside information. James and Caden. Caden's a lion shifter, so I can't see him involved in a group that would sacrifice him. His lion wouldn't like it. James, however, is human. So that puts him at the top of the list. If I can find something that ties him to this group, then we can get out of him who was involved."

Her reasoning made sense, but Kieran still had his doubts.

"He just happened to transfer here right before the killing starts?" she said. "That's suspicious timing."

Kieran went to the desk and shuffled through the files until he found the one he was looking for. "I discussed his transfer with him last night. He had reasons for it," Kieran said. "He's a pretty solid agent." He passed her the file.

"I'm surprised you're not more on my side."

"I'm always on your side. Read the file. I did some digging of my own. If you still think he's in on this, I'll back you. I just don't want you to concentrate your energy on someone that I don't think is involved. You're too good to ignore your instincts, so check James out, but leave room to be wrong about him."

She nodded and took a sip of her coffee. "You trust him?"

Kieran didn't even have to think about his answer. He'd lived by his instincts for years. It was what had kept him going after the ten years he'd spent as a prisoner of the shifters. "Yes, I think I do."

"Okay," she said. "I'll still have Mitch check him out. He can go deeper than this file. Caden too. But I'll keep my options open."

That was his girl. She was always fair and had no problem listening to him. Trusting him. If James was involved and had somehow gotten past Kieran's defenses, he would make the human agent pay. But

Kieran truly believed that James was a good guy, a good agent.

"Five people?" she asked, staring at the board. "Where'd you get that?"

"It was hard to separate the scents in the room, but I was able narrow down enough to pick up six different sweat odors."

"That's incredible," she said. "I couldn't get anything other than blood. Can you tell me more?"

He shook his head. "We'll go back together after Dean and his people are finished. Hopefully, I'll be able to separate more." There was more that he could pick up. The shifters that had held him for those long ten years might have actually done him a favor by messing with his DNA. His already superior senses were enhanced better than anyone or anything in existence.

"Yeah," she said, raising and walking to the board. "We'll try that. I need to get copies of the symbols cut into the skin of our victim. And I need a fucking ID. To see who he is and where they met him."

A knock came from the suite's main door.

"I'll get it," he offered.

She nodded but never took her eyes off the board.

Kieran walked over to the door and opened it for Mitch. The young IT expert, Day Walker and friend had his black hair sporting green highlights this time. Kieran liked the kid and knew if there was anything to dig up on the two new agents, Mitch would find it.

"Hey, man," Kieran greeted. "Thanks for coming."

Mitch grinned at him. "For Dakota? Anytime." He adjusted the strap on his laptop bag.

"Come in." Kieran waved him forward.

Dakota was filling in gaps he'd left open on the timeline, adding what she knew and what she suspected.

"Wow, quite the set-up," Mitch commented. He dropped to his knees next to the coffee table and pulled out his equipment. "Where do you want me to start?"

Kieran just shook his head as Mitch jumped right in. Kieran went to the kitchen and grabbed a cold Coke from the fridge, Mitch's preferred drink. He took it out to Mitch before grabbing his laptop from the desk and sitting on the couch.

"These guys." Kieran wrote down the two newest agents' names and passed the piece of paper to Mitch. "We need to decide if they're involved or can be trusted. I have the basic personnel file but need more."

"No problem," Mitch stated with confidence, his fingers flying across the keys as he typed.

Kieran opened the secured network connection to his company to do his own work. He didn't ask Mitch how the kid would get into the files and didn't want to know. He opened up his email and saw that the others on their team were already responding to the tasks they'd been given.

"How good are the security cameras here?" Dakota asked, turning to them.

"The best," Mitch answered without lifting his head.

"You think Jackson would give us access? The ones at the back door that look across to the apartments?"

"He's aware of the murder," Mitch replied. "Call Alex. I'm sure Jackson already has him working on getting him the info. Hell, they probably know as much as you do at this point."

"I wouldn't be surprised," Dakota picked up her cell and found the right contact name. "This would be too close for Jackson's comfort."

Kieran tuned her out as she spoke to the head of security while he read Dare's first report. The Alpha was pissed, although allowing the agents to do their job. He understood but wanted to talk to Dakota asap.

"Alex already has the tapes. He and Jackson are on their way," she told them.

"Of course they are," Kieran stated. "Damn man can't stay out of the Organization's business. I don't know why he doesn't take a job there."

Mitch giggled, the sound surprising Kieran.

"What?"

"Jackson gives orders, but he doesn't take them," Mitch responded. "He respects your boss, but he won't work for him. Although, since you've gotten here, he's been more involved. He used to let things play out without getting involved as long as it didn't affect his profits."

Kieran nodded. He already knew that. Jackson had built an empire and he deserved everything he'd accomplished. The years they'd spent together as prisoners hadn't been kind to either of them. Still, they'd survived and made something of their lives.

"All I care about is who I can trust," Dakota stated. "I trust you, Jackson and Alex."

"Thanks, Dakota." Mitch wiggled happily. "We trust you too."

Kieran shook his head as Dakota laughed. This was their team. Their friends who would always come when needed. Yeah, he might have been born into a shit family, but he wouldn't trade his chosen family for anything in the world.

Chapter Six

The suite next to theirs had been turned into a conference room and the main point of contact. Dakota wanted to question how Jackson had put everything together so fast, but she wasn't really surprised. Jackson did what he wanted and she just needed to be happy he was still letting her run the investigation.

Besides, after Caspar had shown up and had words with Jackson, she didn't feel like going up against the aggravated Walker, anyway.

Jackson had casually admitted that the room next to theirs was empty and they could get tables and more boards in quickly. That way Kieran and Dakota's space was still their home. The less scents Dakota had to deal with in her residence, the easier her jaguar felt. She appreciated how Jackson recognized that.

Caspar had wanted them to return to the office, but with the crime scene a block away this was where Dakota wanted to be.

Hell, she even had a monitor that was hooked up with Dean's lab so she could see him working in the lab and ask questions as he received results. All in all, it was a fucking badass set-up. Dakota normally hated to be stuck inside when she could be out in the field. Kieran was even worse, but this time Dakota needed to be careful and keep researching. Dean would find what there was to help the investigation on the scene. Dakota needed to find that elusive clue that would lead her to cracking the case.

"You doing okay?"

Dakota didn't turn from the window as Kieran stepped up behind her, his reflection in the tinted glass. "Sure."

"Come on," Kieran urged as he wrapped his arm around her. "Talk to me."

She didn't know what to say, though. Dakota was tired and she was also ready to move on with her life. To spend time with Kieran and her friends. But she knew that things were never going to change. Being in the Organization ensured that as soon as this investigation was over, there would be another one, then another. It didn't matter how tired she was, Dakota had work to do. She always would, until she was behind a desk filing reports from other agents who had taken her place.

"Dakota?" Kieran tightened his hold.

She shook her head. There were too many people in the room who could overhear. Plus, what would it matter if she did complain? There was nothing she could do to avoid her fate.

A few agents in the past had tried to escape the Organization and their duty. Each one had been brought back and gone through reconditioning. They had never been the same after whatever had been done to them.

"Dakota," Dean interrupted through the monitor.

She turned, kissed Kieran's cheek then walked back to the screen. "What's up?"

"Kieran said there were five people involved?" Dean asked.

"Yeah," Kieran answered for himself.

"I think there were six," Dean said.

"Why?" She peered at the monitor, trying to make sense of the data screening over Dean's shoulder. But this wasn't her area of expertise.

"There were no fingerprints," Dean said. "They either wore gloves or cleaned up after themselves. But I did find saliva on the victim."

"Saliva," she repeated. *What the fuck?*

Dean wrinkled his nose in disgust. "Yeah, I think… Jeez, I can't believe I'm about to say this, but I think they licked the blood off the victim after they made the cuts."

"That's gross," Remy said, popping up behind them.

"There's more." Dean cleared his throat. "There were faint traces of semen."

"They raped him?" Dakota asked.

"No," Dean corrected. "I think someone ejaculated over his body."

Okay, that was creepier that the saliva. "I didn't see anything in the other investigation files about that."

"There isn't." Mitch spoke up. "I've read the older cases three times today and there was nothing on the other victims. Not saliva or semen. In fact, the previous bodies were bathed and cleaned for the rituals. The last lab tech did find a trace of soap he suspected was used. He tried to trace where the soap had been purchased, but it was one of the most common brands. Just everyday household soap." Mitch passed Dakota the file.

Dakota flipped through the lab reports, not really reading the words. She trusted Mitch. "So why is this time different?"

"I don't know," Dean confessed. "I'm just giving you the facts right now. You need to decide what they mean." He grinned at her.

"Bastard," she teased.

"Hey! I'm letting you have all the fun," Dean responded.

"Appreciate it, buddy," she snarked. "Now get back to work."

Dean sent her a sharp salute before turning his back and returning to his laptop.

"What do you think this means?" Remy asked.

Dakota opened her mouth to tell him she didn't know when Kieran spoke.

"It's not the same people," Kieran stated.

She jerked her gaze over to her lover. "What do you mean?"

"We've been assuming that the crimes are all connected. That they've all been done by the same group of people," Kieran said.

Dakota nodded.

"I don't think they are," Kieran told her.

"They have to be," she argued. "The symbols, the way the bodies are found, how they start with animal rituals and move on to humans then shifters —"

"I know." Kieran held up his hand. "But there has to be another explanation. The only ones who would be able to know the details would be shifters or another paranormal."

"Right," she agreed.

"But why would a shifter sacrifice another shifter?" Kieran asked.

"For the same reason a shifter attacks another?" Remy questioned. "We deal with that almost every day."

"True. And I can't explain it, but my gut is telling me that this is something different. We're on the wrong path," Kieran said.

In all the time they'd been together Dakota had never not trusted Kieran. She wasn't going to start now. "Okay," she said. "So where do we begin?"

Kieran shuffled his feet. "I don't know."

Dakota laughed. He looked like a little boy who'd just done something wrong.

"If I'm not right, I could be holding back the investigation," he continued,

"And if you're right, we might be able to actually solve this case before someone else dies," Dakota pointed out. She gestured to a blank white board. "That one, we need to put only the information we know about this case. Forget anything we've read from the other files. Just facts about the Vegas rituals."

"I'll do it." Mitch hopped up from where he'd been sitting on the floor. "I've read the notes most recently."

"Good. Thanks." Dakota turned to Remy. "We need to re-interview Damon. This time listen to what he has to say about ritual sites and not what we think we know."

"I'm on it," Remy said.

"Go now," she ordered. "Gabe and Dare should still be there. Get them to help. I'll call Damon as soon as I can and talk to him."

"What about me?" Kieran asked.

Dakota pulled him back toward the window where they wouldn't be in front of the monitor. "I need you to be completely honest with me and yourself. Can we trust James? What is your gut telling you?"

He pressed his lips together before finally nodding.

She stomped back over to the monitor. "James?"

The human agent appeared in front of where Dean was working.

"Meet me and Kieran back at the scene. I want to take another look. This time with a new set of eyes. You haven't been inside, right?"

"No, I haven't," he answered.

"Good, just concentrate on this scene. Nothing else."

"I can do that," James told her.

"Good," Dakota said. "We'll see you there." She turned to Kieran. "Let's go."

He was already headed toward the door. Dakota fell in step behind him until they'd exited the room and were heading to the elevator.

"Thanks for trusting me," Kieran whispered.

Dakota slipped her hand in his. "I always will." She squeezed his fingers.

The elevator door opened and they stepped inside.

As soon as the doors had closed, he turned to her.

"I need to tell you something," he said.

Dakota's stomach churned. The look on his face was full of regret. "Okay."

"While you were at the office yesterday, I was downstairs. I met up with Alex and we grabbed a cup of coffee. He had to leave, so I decided to sit at one of the tables. There was a young girl there."

Dakota stumbled back against the wall. *No, no.* Kieran wouldn't betray her like that.

"She came up to the table and sat. No one talks to me. You know that. But this girl...she just sat down and began to talk."

Why was he telling her this now? Dakota was about to be sick. Kieran had turned so she could only see his profile. She wanted to beat him with her fists, but that wouldn't accomplish anything.

"I know I should have told you before, but I didn't know how. I kept telling myself that when the time was right I'd confess, but you were working this case —"

"Stop," she spat out. "Just stop."

"Dakota," he said.

"Don't!" She was going to shake apart.

"No!" he roared. He grabbed her then yanked her forward. "Never!"

Tears were falling.

"Baby." He cupped her face. "Look at me."

She raised her eyes to meet his. As soon as Dakota processed what he was telling her, she was going to kill him.

"I would never cheat on you," he stated. "Never."

"What?"

"Who. Your niece," he blurted out. "Your niece was at the hotel looking for you. Or she found you and couldn't approach. Scared, I guess. Anyway, she asked me to tell you. But there was so much going on and I didn't know how to bring it up."

Dakota sagged against her lover. She was absolutely going to murder him. After she could breathe, that was. "You didn't sleep with her?" She just had to make sure.

"Fuck, no," he growled. "I can't believe you'd even ask me that."

"I wouldn't have twenty minutes ago. Before this conversation." She pulled out of his arms before punching him in the chest. "You fucker! What the hell?"

"Ow! Shit, that hurt." Kieran rubbed his chest.

"Why would you even talk like that?" she yelled. "I thought you'd slept with someone else."

"I get that now," Kieran bitched.

She was so pissed off that she went to hit him again until someone cleared their throat behind them. Dakota whirled around and came face to face with Alex.

"You've already scared off everyone in the close vicinity, but I would prefer not to have to clean blood from the carpet," Alex said.

Damn it, the elevator had reached the ground level and Alex was holding the door open. She growled at Kieran, her jaguar close to the surface, then stalked out on to the main floor of the hotel. "Sorry."

Alex nodded. "Completely understandable." He glared at Kieran. "I only heard the last bit, but I suspect Kieran deserves whatever you do to him."

"Thanks a lot," Kieran muttered.

"I need to get back to work," Dakota said. She didn't stop to wait for Kieran. Fresh air sounded good about then. She pushed out through the door and inhaled deeply.

"I'm sorry," Kieran said from behind her.

Dakota nodded. She knew he was.

"It's just that you trust me so completely and I was hiding this from you," Kieran told her. "I couldn't do it any longer."

Hell, he hadn't managed to do it for more than twenty-four hours. She smiled, although she remained with her back to him. Her reaction had been over the top, but that was her jaguar pushing to come out. The thought of their mate being with someone else was enough for Dakota to almost shift. Kieran belonged to her and her jaguar and no one was going to get in the way of that.

Shifters were normally protective of their mates. Just because Dakota and Kieran hadn't taken the final step in sealing their bond didn't mean that Dakota wouldn't kill for her mate.

But that line of thought just reminded her that she could still lose him. If not to his father, then to someone else. She'd told Kieran that they could wait to have any discussions about mating until they were more settled, but she didn't know how much longer they could go like this.

"Dakota?"

"I love you," she told him.

"God, I love you too. I'm so sorry."

"No, I am." She turned and faced the man who meant everything to her. The only person that wasn't with her because he didn't have any other choice. Kieran chose to be with her. "I shouldn't have jumped to conclusions."

"I didn't say it right—"

"Stop, Kieran," she said. "This is my fault."

"No, I should've—"

She took two steps forward so she could grab the front of his shirt and hold him close. "I want to mate you."

* * * *

Kieran stared at her as Dakota's words echoed in his mind. He knew that was what she wanted, what she'd always wanted. Dakota's jaguar had left him unmated for longer than anyone had expected.

He had his reasons why he hadn't said yes, the years of being held and tortured at the hands of shifters being only one. Kieran still didn't think he was good enough for her. Dakota deserved so much more than a broken man who couldn't sleep in the dark alone.

Looking in her eyes, though, he could see how much she loved him. How she'd fight for him even if she had to fight him.

"Okay." The words were simple, but he meant them with all his heart. Kieran would be hers and she would belong to him. A true partnership in every sense.

She scrunched her nose as she jerked. "Okay?"

"Okay, I will mate with you. I love you and I'll never leave you."

Her eyes filled but this time he could see the happiness that flowed from her. "I…I…"

"Let me kiss you," he said.

She rose to her tiptoes then slammed her mouth on his. Dakota kissed him and it was perfect and what he needed.

Kieran slid his hands down her back, pressing her against his body. "Mine," he whispered when they broke apart.

"Mate," she said.

"Mate," he repeated.

"I want to take you upstairs and do it now," she told him.

Kieran chuckled. He wanted the same thing. "Too bad we have work to do."

"Yeah." She sighed.

"But as soon as we close the case, we can take a few days, stay in our suite and you can bite me, claim me," he reminded her. Okay, he was reminding himself too, since once he'd actually agreed to mate with her, he'd have everything he wanted.

He wanted to walk around with the mating mark, so all shifters knew that he had been claimed by such an amazing woman.

"That wasn't nice at all," she complained.

"Let's go." He took her hand and led her across the parking lot. The crime scene was still taped off and two uniformed police officers guarding the area. "About your niece…"

"It's okay," she said. "We'll discuss it later. Right now, we should concentrate on this investigation."

Kieran was certain that Dakota was putting off even thinking about her niece. He'd known how hard it would be to face that part of her life. Hell, her parents hadn't even celebrated her birthdays or spent any time with her for the few years that Dakota had lived with them. No emotional connection. That was what they'd explained to her. How a girl of five was supposed to live with the knowledge that her parents didn't love her was beyond him. In his opinion, they didn't deserve to know her. Not even now. And he felt the same about Kayla.

That young girl might want to know about the Organization, but did she really have that right? She'd been raised with a family that had taken care of her. Kayla had been given everything that Dakota had not.

If Dakota didn't want to deal with this new development of her family, then Kieran would do what he could to distract her. Besides, he'd kept his word. Kieran had told Dakota that Kayla wanted to see her. It was Dakota's decision whether she wanted to follow up with the girl.

"Why'd you want James to meet us?" Kieran asked, to get her mind back on the investigation.

"I thought you read his file."

"I did," he responded. Okay, she knew him well. "I skimmed it."

"As a human agent, he was sent to the FBI training academy. He also spent five years working alongside the human police force before being assigned to his last post. He has more experience on the homicide side of our case. I want him to work that angle while we look at groups that might be responsible."

"That's a great idea," he praised. Kieran was a man of action. One that enjoyed being out in the field cracking heads. He never wanted to have to sit behind a desk and be responsible for figuring out what to do next. Still, being able to work with Dakota was always a good time.

"James should be here soon, but let's go ahead and go inside. I want you to do a walk through and see if you can pick up anything else," she said.

"Sure."

The young officer at the bottom of the stairwell nodded to them. "Agent Smith, Agent Reese."

"We have another agent on the way. No one else is to come up," Dakota said.

"Yes, ma'am."

The young officer was nervous, but Kieran could tell it was tinged with respect. Since the Organization didn't exist on paper, the local cops dealing with them merely knew they were a federal agency. Kieran didn't know how Caspar got away with that, but they'd never had any trouble.

"Thank you," Dakota told the officer. She led the way upstairs and Kieran followed.

The entire complex was empty. That meant that whoever was responsible for the events of last night had had their choice of which unit to use. There had to be some reason for the choice of that particular unit. He paused at the door of the apartment and spun then walked to the rail.

Across the parking lot, over the rows of vehicles, was the door that Kieran and Dakota had just exited. He believed now more than ever that the location where the victim had been found was quite deliberate. Which meant the entire scene had been a set-up.

He peered around, taking in each and every sight within his vision. No one was paying extra attention to what they were doing. Sure, humans passed by and looked curious, but they quickly moved on. Still Kieran felt like he was missing something.

Inside the apartment, Dakota was walking around and muttering to herself. Their connection and his senses allowed him to follow her progress. He needed to get in there and help, but he couldn't make his feet move.

He didn't jump when his cell in his pocket began to ring. No, he expected it.

Kieran pulled the phone from his pocket. The caller ID said *unknown* but he had no doubt who was calling him.

"Hello, Father," Kieran answered.

Dakota stopped moving around. Of course she would be able to hear. Kieran wasn't hiding anything from her though.

"Kieran," the Elder Argent responded. "You're looking well."

He looked around again but still didn't see anything out of the ordinary. He definitely didn't spot his father. "I'm feeling good. Can't complain. Where are you?"

"Close," his father replied. "Just waiting for you to come to me."

"Tell me where you are and I'll be right there," Kieran promised.

"You're not ready," his father said. "When you are, I won't have to tell you where I am."

Dakota skimmed her hand down his shoulder, giving him the strength he needed. "I don't care where you are. I already told you that I want nothing to do with you."

"That isn't a choice you get to make. You were born of my blood. The things we will do together are going to be fabulous."

"We're not doing anything together," Kieran corrected. "Leave. I'll give you one chance to leave. If you contact me again, if I see you, or you come after anyone I care about, I will destroy you."

"Spoken like a true Argent."

"I'm not an Argent," Kieran snapped. "Never will be."

"We'll see," his father said. "In the meantime, I'll enjoy watching you work, I think. Although I've been disappointed so far."

Kieran growled. "If you have anything to do with this—"

His father laughed. "You'll what? Besides, I wasn't even in town when that young man was killed. My contacts have informed me on every step of your investigation. Or should I say your lover's investigation."

"Leave her out of this," Kieran ordered. "This is between me and you."

"I wish I could. However, I've been given the impression that she's the one who holds you to this place. To these people. I'll do what I have to do."

Kieran turned to see Dakota. She should be able to hear both sides of the conversation.

Kieran shook his head, but Dakota was smiling.

She faced the rail like he had been and lifted her middle finger into the air taunting his father.

"Charming." His father sounded as though he'd swallowed something sour.

"Yes, she is," Kieran agreed.

"Get rid of her or I will."

His father hung up right as a black SUV came barreling down the alley.

Kieran had just enough time to leap at Dakota and knock her down. He covered her body with his as a rain of bullets rained above them.

With a squeal of tires, the SUV rounded the corner.

"Move!" Dakota pushed at his chest.

Kieran rolled off her. Dakota was on her feet and racing down the steps before he had a chance to blink. Instead of following her, he jumped over the rail and landed on the sidewalk next to the officer who'd been taking cover.

The officer flinched, going for his weapon.

"It's okay," Kieran told him. "Are you hit?"

"No, sir, I'm fine." The officer looked toward where the other had been stationed. "Freddy?" he yelled.

"I'm good," Freddy shouted back. "Saw the guns and got my ass down."

"Good man," Kieran called. He patted the young officer on the shoulder then took off at a sprint. He wouldn't be able to catch the SUV, but maybe he could get a glimpse at the license plate or the men.

He was surprised that Dakota wasn't following him, but he knew she was uninjured. He hadn't smelt any blood. Kieran used every bit of speed he had, trying to catch up. He covered the first block easily. Up ahead the traffic would be brutal and he needed to get to the corner.

In less than a minute it was obvious he hadn't been quick enough. Kieran slowed down and stopped once he reached the main street. There was just too much traffic to try to find a black SUV in the sea of vehicles.

"Fuck," he spat. Kieran turned around and began the walk back toward the apartments. He yanked out his phone and hit the number for Mitch.

"Already working on the cameras," Mitch said instead of a standard greeting.

"How?"

"Dakota called. Alex and Jackson are with her and the human officers. Jackson wanted to make sure the shooters didn't circle back around."

"Damn it, I didn't think of that," Kieran bitched. It would be just like his father to use a distraction tactic. Kieran needed to get his head in the game.

"Caspar is checking the local flights to see if your dad flew commercial or private. He said he had people watching for him and hadn't been notified."

"He wouldn't have used his own name," Kieran stated.

"Doesn't matter," Mitch said. "If Caspar doesn't find him, then I will."

"Thanks." Kieran saved his strength and walked back, knowing that Jackson and Alex wouldn't let anything happen to Dakota.

His father might have won round one, but that just motivated Kieran further.

When he reached the apartments, not only were Jackson and Alex there with Dakota, but James had arrived as well. He ignored the men and went straight to his lover.

She was ready for him. Dakota went right into his arms as he pulled her forward. "I'm okay," she murmured. "I'm okay."

He nodded with his face buried in her shoulder. He might not crave her scent like a shifter, but Kieran did crave her. Holding her close, he just closed his eyes and was grateful that she was still there with him.

"I'll kill him," Kieran whispered to her. "I'm going to fucking destroy him."

She pulled back and grinned at him. "I hope you'll at least let me watch."

Kieran laughed. "Oh no, baby," he teased. "You owe him some of your own for shooting at you."

"And that's why I love you."

"I could have lost you," Kieran said. "I never want to feel that way again."

"Then let's finish what we're here to do and get this case solved."

"Yeah." He let her go and headed over to Jackson and Alex.

Jackson followed Dakota with his eyes as she walked up the stairs to the apartment before he looked back to Kieran. "She's fine. Pissed, but I think that might help her until she can get back home."

"I appreciate you two coming and watching over her," Kieran said.

"Of course," Jackson responded. "Although I'd like a piece of your father myself. Dakota told us what he said."

"He claims he doesn't have anything to do with the murder, but I don't believe him. Even if he has contacts in town, the entire situation makes me sick."

"You father might have connections, but they won't be nearly as good as mine," Jackson said. "We'll find him."

"Yeah, the sooner the better. He won't stop at one attempt on Dakota. If he thinks she's what's holding me here, he won't stop until she's taken out of the equation."

"How he thinks that will win you over to his side is beyond me," Alex said.

Kieran snorted. "My father doesn't understand love. He surely can't comprehend what losing Dakota would do to me."

"We'll concentrate on tracking him down. You get this mess finished with. I don't want that kind of evil anywhere near my place." Jackson motioned toward the apartment.

"You got it." Kieran waved to Jackson and Alex one last time before stomping up the stairs.

There were more cops surrounding the area now with the shooting that had taken place.

Luckily, he recognized some agents from the office who seemed to be handling the situation. *What a hell of a day and it isn't over yet.* Kieran had to go back in the apartment.

Inside Dakota was laying out her plan to James about him taking on the homicide portion. They'd run joint investigations, hoping that the two sides would lead to the group.

She waved Kieran inside as he stepped up to the threshold.

The scent of blood was still strong, even with the body taken to the morgue. He walked over to the spot where the body had been placed. The young man had been killed where he'd been found.

Kieran squatted down and placed his hand where the poor kid's chest had been. The stained concrete served as a reminder that while they wanted the case closed, they also needed to get justice for the innocent man. Whoever he was, he didn't deserve to die the way he had.

He was still only picking up five scents, although there was one weird odor he was getting. It was almost like someone had been attempting to cover their trace. Was that baking soda? Something Kieran recognized but wasn't able to place.

"We have a name," Dakota said behind him.

Kieran rose.

"Matt Watts, student at UNLV." She was reading from her phone. "He'd only been here a couple of months. Jesus, eighteen years old from Colorado."

"Matt." Kieran repeated the name. Their victim had been identified and should be called by his name.

"His roommate contacted campus police when Matt didn't come home from a study session," Dakota told them.

"I'd like to get to the roommate right away," James said. "See his room."

"Yeah, go." She turned to Kieran. "I want to shift."

"Okay, why don't you go into the bathroom? Leave the door open. I'll keep everyone out."

Dakota smiled at him. "That way they don't see me naked?"

He was a possessive bastard. Dakota knew that. "I can stand here naked if it makes you feel better."

Predictably, she growled. "I don't think so." She eyed him but went toward the bathroom.

Kieran strode so he was standing in the doorway. No one would be able to see him and he wouldn't allow anyone through.

He heard his lover begin her transformation but didn't turn until she padded back into the main room. Kieran allowed her to sniff her way across the room to him.

As always, she'd seek him out first when in her jaguar form.

Kieran lowered to his knees so she could run her muzzle across his chest and up his neck. Before he'd met her, Kieran would never have allowed a shifter this close. He didn't have to worry anymore, though. Dakota would hurt herself before she'd hurt him.

"Hello, beautiful," he said, rubbing his palms over her chin. "That's it, yes, mark me. I'm yours." Kieran didn't pick up scents and carry them, a legacy of his Walker genes, but Dakota's animal nature would still need to claim what was hers.

She pulled back and he rose.

"Now get to work," he said. "Sexy time later."

Dakota gave his hand a long lick with her rough tongue. Damn, he did not enjoy that and she knew it.

"Great." He wiped his hand on his jeans. "Kitty drool."

She yowled at him as she took a swipe at him with her claws in.

Even on a shit day, Dakota could make him laugh.

Chapter Seven

Dakota let the hot water cascade down her shoulders onto her back. She was wrecked and didn't know how much more she could give. After spending an hour in her shifted form, she'd returned to the work suite and pored through reports.

Jackson had insisted on bringing up dinner from one of his restaurants and they'd dined on steak and all the fixings while huddled around the conference table. She had to admit that having a good meal had kept her fueled to get through the worst of the paperwork. But when the clock had reached midnight, it hadn't just been her that had been dragging. She'd finally had to send everyone home so they could get some rest.

James had stayed in one of the bedrooms of the work suite, with Remy taking the other. Having the team close by helped make her feel secure enough for the long steaming-hot shower.

She didn't know when Kieran's father would strike next, but she was certain it would be soon.

The group they were hunting also seemed to know all about them. They knew where the main investigators were and had mocked them. The need to make sure her mate was safe had the jaguar inside her on edge. Dakota turned off the water and opened the shower stall door. Kieran stood on the mat in nothing but his low-riding pajama pants while holding her towel.

"Why didn't you join me?" she asked.

He stepped forward and started to dry her off. "I was going to, but Damon called. He's calmed down and had some new ideas. He's going to send you an email and come by a little later to see how he can help."

"What'd he say?" she questioned. "I know he told you." It felt nice to let him pamper her.

Kieran shook his head. "Tomorrow." He laughed. "Or later this morning. We both need sleep and nothing he has to say is going to change anything tonight."

She had to agree. Her mind felt like mush and she wanted just a few uninterpreted hours of sleep. Actually, there was one thing she wanted more.

"How are you going to distract me?" she asked, running the tips of her fingers above the waistband of his pants.

"I can think of a few ways." Kieran dropped the towel before he picked her up.

"Kieran!"

"Hush, let me take care of you," he told her.

It had really shaken him when they'd been shot at. Her lover wasn't concerned about himself but instead for her. "Okay, baby." She teased him with his own words.

She expected him to toss her onto the mattress as he was prone to do, but he surprised her by setting her gently in the middle of the bed. He'd already pulled the covers down so the cool soft sheets against her bare body made her shiver.

"I'll warm you up," he promised. Kieran pulled off his pants, revealing his amazing body to her.

Once she was able to claim him as her mate, he'd have a bite mark on his shoulder that would never fully heal. It wouldn't be the only scar his strong body held. While normally a Walker wouldn't have any blemish, the years of torture had taken their toll on her lover's body. He was still perfect in her eyes, though.

"What are you thinking about?" he asked as he stroked his thick erection.

"How absolutely edible you are," she told him. "Why don't you come closer, so I can do that for you?"

He grinned but remained standing next to the bed, jacking himself.

"Please," she begged. Kieran liked when she pleaded with him and Dakota was ready to do anything she could to get him to join her.

"Touch yourself," he ordered. "Show me how much you want me."

Oh, he wants a show? I'll give him a show. Dakota ran her right hand down her side while cupping her breast with the left. "Touch myself?" she purred. "Well, I guess I'll have to if you won't do it for me."

His pupils dilated, but still he refused to give in.

Dakota brushed the fingers of her right hand over her thigh before making her way to her pussy. She spread her legs so Kieran was getting the perfect view as she circled her clit.

There was no way she could hold in the moan.

Having Kieran's gaze, burning and bright, on her was crazy hot.

He licked his lips and she licked hers.

Kieran used his thumb to collect the drop of pre-cum from the tip of his shaft. Dakota slipped her middle finger through her wet folds and teased herself.

"More," he demanded.

He stroked faster. She plunged her finger deep.

"Faster," he ordered.

As he sped up his own hand, Dakota lifted her hips so she could thrust. She added a second digit, her ecstasy ramping up and passion flowing like her juices.

Kieran was like a golden god as he pumped his body to meet his steady rhythm.

It took everything in her to keep her eyes open. She wanted to watch her lover as his gaze remained focused on her.

She cried out and that was what broke Kieran.

He leapt onto the bed. Slamming his mouth down on hers, he thrust his tongue inside as he pulled her hand away and replaced her fingers with his. Her entire body was buzzing.

Kieran lifted his head and snarled. "Mine!"

"Yes!" she hissed.

Using his knees to open her farther, he positioned his cock at her entrance.

Dakota raised her hips up and off the mattress so the tip of his shaft pressed inside. She gripped his back as she bowed. "Take me. Please!"

With one strong solid plunge, he was finally inside her.

"Kieran!" she shouted to her lover.

"Fuck!" he roared. On the verge of losing control, Kieran rode her hard.

"Please! More!" she urged him on.

The sweat on both their bodies had hands slipping off and legs sliding against each other but that didn't hold either of them back. They were like animals rutting and devouring. It was honest and remarkable.

It wasn't very often that she got to see this side of him.

The power that poured from him enveloped her.

Her jaguar surged to the forefront and she had to push the animal back.

"Kieran, I'm—"

He sat back, pulling her up onto his lap. The new angle had him sliding deeper.

Dakota screamed as she was overwhelmed by her desire. She closed her eyes while dropping her head back. Letting him control every inch of her was a release in itself. But her climax was coming and all she could do was hold on for dear life.

Thrusting and cursing, Kieran took her higher and higher until she gasped for breath and orgasmed. It hit her so hard that she felt dizzy for a moment. He lay her back on the mattress, never slowing down.

Dakota clung to him as he chased his own release.

She dug her nails into the solid muscles of his back and arched.

He came with one last bellow.

In the sudden silence and through the ringing in her ears, she could barely hear the words he murmured against her neck.

Sweet and soft expressions of how much he loved her.

With the feeling of safety as well as the solid presence of the man who'd be her mate warming her, Dakota closed her eyes and let herself drift to sleep.

* * * *

This couldn't be happening.

There was no possible way that her phone ringing was waking her for the second morning in a row. Dakota rolled over and reached for the annoying little device as Kieran began to growl beside her.

"I hate whoever is calling you," Kieran bitched.

Dakota couldn't agree more.

"Who is it?" he demanded.

She rubbed her eyes, trying to bring the screen into focus. "It's the front desk." Why in the hell would the front desk be calling? Dakota slid her finger over her phone. "Hello."

"I'm so sorry to bother you, Ms. Reese, but we have someone at the front desk who is demanding access to your floor. In fact, security had to stop her from stealing the elevator pass from another guest."

Dakota glanced over at Kieran who could hear what was said on both sides of the call.

"Who is it? What does she want?" Dakota demanded.

"That's the thing," the receptionist told her. "She won't answer. Won't give us a name. I didn't know if it would be better to call you or get the head of security."

Alex had been up with them, so he needed his sleep. Dakota didn't want him bothered. She slung off the covers before throwing her legs over the side of the bed. "No, it's okay. I'm sorry this person caused you trouble. I'll be right down."

"Thank you, ma'am."

The call was disconnected.

"You're not going alone," Kieran told her. He was still lying in bed.

"Want me to wake Remy? Or James? They're in the next suite."

He growled. "Funny."

No, what was funny was Kieran sighing and bitching as he climbed out of bed and stomped to the closest. He wasn't a morning person. Especially when they'd only gotten a few hours' sleep.

She glanced at the clock. Damn, three hours was all they'd managed. It was only a few minutes before four in the morning.

"I'm sure it's nothing," Dakota said as she pulled on a pair of jeans.

"Because so much in our life is easy?"

Okay, so he had a point there.

"It's inside one of the busiest hotels and casinos in the city."

He snorted.

Since there was no way to talk him out of going downstairs with her, Dakota walked to the bathroom. She had a bad feeling that she wasn't going to back to sleep anytime soon.

They were quiet as they finished getting ready and into the elevator. As the exited onto the main floor, Kieran's scowl had the few people around scattering out of his path.

The made their way through the maze of table games and slot machines until they had a clear view of the reception area.

"You've got to be fucking kidding me," Kieran spat.

Dakota stopped. "What?"

"That's your niece."

Standing between two large men in black suits was a young girl wearing ripped jeans and a black long-sleeved shirt. Dakota narrowed her eyes. "That's the girl who smiled at me at the scene earlier."

"Jesus Christ," he growled.

Well, this hadn't been how she'd hoped to start her day, but once again the hands of fate gave her no choice but to deal.

Dakota stalked forward, keeping her eye on the teenager who had come to town looking for her. Dakota had once wished to know the family she'd been born into. That had passed as the years had gone by and she'd been working for the Organization.

This girl, who'd had the luck of not being a firstborn, was throwing everything Dakota lived for away but breaking the rules of the Organization. She wanted to know her aunt? Well, Dakota didn't have anything to say to her. Dakota wasn't like the rest of her family and never would be. Not only were there rules that she had to abide by, but Dakota felt no connection to this stranger.

She stopped toe to toe with the girl. "I can have them arrest you," she said. "Is that what you wanted?"

The girl frowned. "I'm Kayla."

"I don't need to know your name, although I'm sure the cops would appreciate it."

Kayla glanced at Kieran. "Didn't you tell her? You said you would?"

Instead of answering, Kieran crossed his arms over his chest.

Kayla sighed before looking back at Dakota. "I needed to talk to you."

"At four in the morning?"

"Yes, I had to—"

"You didn't have to come to my home, try to steal a key card or break into an elevator," Dakota stated. "Those were choices you made."

"It was an emergency," Kayla argued.

Dakota was tired and fed up with this bullshit. "What. Do. You. Want."

"I told you, I need to talk to you." She peered around to the security. "In private."

"No," Dakota responded. She turned to the security guards. "Call the police."

"It's about what happened this morning," Kayla called out after Dakota had started walking away.

Dakota stopped. She'd been trying not to think about anything, but yeah, that girl had been at the scene of a murder. She'd seemed to know that Dakota would be there. "Shit." She rubbed her hand over her face. *Can this get any uglier?*

"I can have her escorted out of here to wait for the police," Kieran offered.

She shook her head. While she had no trouble turning her back on a spoiled brat, Dakota did need to know what this teenager knew about the murder. "I'm going to have to talk to her. She was at the scene this morning and if she claims to know something—"

"I'll talk to her or go get James. He's running the homicide investigation after all," Kieran said. "It doesn't have to be you."

But it did. The ache in her chest as she peered at the girl wasn't going to go away until she'd dealt with Kayla. Dakota hated that she still felt hurt by the way her family had frozen her out of their loves. She'd been trying to push the feeling down and bury it, but seeing Kayla there brought back the pain. Dakota hadn't been loved, but this girl surely had been.

Life wasn't always fair. Dakota hadn't chosen the path she was on, but if she hadn't been born into the Organization, she wouldn't have met Kieran. She could be mated to another shifter, with children, and working for one of the family companies. That wasn't how she saw her life playing out, though.

"I'll talk to her then have Caspar contact the family. They can come pick her up, or we'll have some agents return her home. No matter what, I want her out of this city," Dakota demanded.

"I can help with that."

She turned as Jackson and Alex strode up. "What are you doing here? Don't you sleep?"

Jackson laughed. "I could ask the same about the two of you. As hard as my staff tries not to bother me with what they consider below my attention, I do know what's going on in my place."

Kieran grinned. "I'm sure there are a few things that get by you." The evil glint in his eyes had Dakota wondering what her mate had planned.

"Trust me. I know more than you think." Jackson winked. "When's the mating taking place?"

Kieran's mouth dropped open as Dakota stepped back.

Chuckling, Jackson nodded.

"Smartass," Kieran muttered.

"Yes," Jackson agreed. "But before you compliment me further, why don't we get this little matter into a more private location?" Jackson waved his security guards forward. "Please take the young lady up to Conference room C. We'll join you shortly."

Kayla didn't argue as she was taken away. She did, however, grin at Dakota, apparently pleased that she'd gotten her way. Dakota didn't know whether to laugh or strangle the girl. Did her niece have any idea on how badly she was fucking with the system? And what exactly was her involvement with the ritual sacrifices?

Dakota would have known if Kayla had been in the room. Not only would she have smelt another jaguar shifter, but a member of her own clan as well.

"I'm texting Remy. Have him and James meet us," Kieran said.

"Fine," Dakota agreed. "No reason anyone else should get any more sleep."

"How about we grab some coffee from the shop?" Jackson offered. "I'll escort you to the conference room after."

Dakota glanced over at her shoulder as Jackson led her away. Alex had a hold of Kieran's arm, talking softly to him. Either Alex wanted to talk to Kieran or Jackson wished to talk to her.

The coffee shop was empty of any other patrons. The casino was still bustling with people, but nowhere near as many as there would be in a short few hours. The sleepy-looking barista straightened as soon as he spotted Jackson.

"Sir!" the barista said. "Good morning. Your usual?"

Jackson nodded in greeting. "Good morning, Bryan. Yes, I would like my usual, plus can you make an additional six?"

"Yes, sir."

Jackson turned to her. "Or would you like something other than the house blend?"

"That's fine," Dakota agreed. She peered out the entrance at where Kieran was no longer standing.

"Why don't we sit while Bryan finishes our order?"

Dakota strode over to a table close by and sat. Jackson's amusement was evident as he joined her.

"What did you want to talk about?" she asked. There was no point in playing games. Plus, she did consider Jackson a friend.

"I'm worried about Kieran," he stated boldly.

She lifted an eyebrow in response.

"His father is toying with him. Trying to catch Kieran off his game," Jackson continued.

Dakota nodded.

"If I get the chance, I'm going to take him out. Even if he doesn't do anything to Kieran."

Well that was blunt. "Why are you telling me?"

"Because it will be your job to arrest me for killing a Walker when it isn't in self-defense," Jackson said.

"You want to get arrested?"

"No," Jackson said. "I'm sure my lawyers would get me off a murder charge anyway. Or Alex will set the scene to ensure that it does get ruled as self-defense. Either way, I won't spend a night in one of your cells."

Dakota splayed out her hands in a gesture for more information.

"You, however, don't have the same resources as I do," Jackson told her. "Your Organization would give you up in a second if they had to. We both know that the power and connections that Kieran's father has could be an issue. He's a man who's made friends in some places. He already has some business associates believing Kieran is on board."

"Well, they'll be disappointed when Kieran doesn't join the family, won't they?"

"More than disappointed. From our research, we've found out that Kieran's father has gotten in over his head with some dangerous people. He needs Kieran's power."

"He won't get Kieran or his power," Dakota declared.

"No, he won't," Jackson agreed.

"Your order is ready sir," Bryan called.

Jackson lifted a hand in acknowledgment before he leaned across the table toward her. "I'm asking you to let me handle Kieran's father. Please. I can protect him and you. I know it will be hard —"

"Hard?" Dakota interrupted. "My jaguar wants to hunt him down and rip out his throat."

"Yeah, I bet," Jackson said. "But I'm asking, let me do this for my oldest friend."

It was a lot to ask of her. Dakota understood, though, that it had been Jackson next to Kieran in the hellish cells they'd been held in. If Kieran's father hadn't thrown Kieran out into the world with no money, contacts or knowledge of how things worked, Kieran wouldn't have been captured. But Kieran was hers. The person that completed both her and the animal inside. To give this to Jackson was allowing someone else to protect her mate. Every instinct she had was screaming at her to warn Jackson off.

Even if she went down for killing Kieran's father, Dakota wouldn't care as long as her mate was safe.

"If you go to prison or, God forbid, get killed, I'll lose my best friend," Jackson whispered. "He'll go insane and you know it. He'll never stop revenging you and no one else will be able to reach him."

Dakota sighed. "I want to talk to him before you kill him."

Jackson opened his mouth, but Dakota held up her hand.

"If possible," she added. "If you can and do capture him, I want to see him. Then I'll let you do whatever it is you have planned."

Jackson laid his palm over the hand she was resting on the table. He squeezed and nodded. "I swear I'll try to give that to you."

"Then let's get upstairs so we can get this investigation finished and concentrate on protecting Kieran," Dakota said.

"He won't like it," Jackson told her.

"I know."

They rose and Jackson strode to the counter. He didn't pay for their coffees—he did own the place—but he slipped a twenty-dollar bill into the tip jar.

"Thank you, Bryan," Jackson said to the young barista.

"Thank you," Bryan responded. "If you need another round, just let me know. I get off in thirty minutes and I could drop it off to your office on my way out."

Jackson nodded, but there was a faint blush on his cheeks.

Dakota waited at the entrance and smirked.

"Shut up," Jackson told her after handing her one of the carriers.

"Are you sleeping with the barista?" she asked. Dakota didn't care, but it was cute the way the barista sighed as he watched Jackson's ass.

"Of course not," Jackson snapped. "He works for me."

"Uh-huh."

"He has a crush on me," Jackson said.

"I noticed."

"Can we not talk about it?" Jackson asked.

Dakota shrugged. "It's funny to see you all flustered."

"I am not flustered," Jackson growled. "I am one of the most powerful beings in the world."

"Who just got flustered because some young twink was checking him out," Dakota teased.

"You were a lot nicer before Kieran corrupted you," Jackson said.

They reached the private elevator that led to the business levels where Jackson worked. Dakota waited as Jackson used the palm of his hand to grant them access.

Once they were enclosed in the privacy of the elevator, Dakota turned to her mate's best friend. "He's one of a kind, isn't he?"

Jackson nodded. "I look at his father and the rest of his family, trying to see some good in them. How could Kieran have come from such an awful clan?"

"I don't know much about the other Argents," Dakota admitted. "I've been concentrating on his father."

"I'll let you read the files," Jackson offered. "Just don't show them to Kieran. There's things in there he doesn't need to know."

The doors opened and Dakota followed Jackson out and down the hall. Kieran hadn't looked into his family, as far as Dakota knew. He'd never gone back home or sought out anyone. When he'd been sent from his home, that had been the end for Kieran.

In one of their late-night talks, Kieran had confessed that when he'd first been taken, he'd believed his father had been behind it. A test. A way for his father to gauge if Kieran was strong enough. Kieran didn't know how long he'd held that belief, but as the years had passed slowly, he'd turned to hoping that his father would rescue him. Kieran had been wishing for a hero.

Help had come to Kieran after ten years, but it had been Caspar who'd saved him.

Kieran's father hadn't cared what had happened until word had gotten back to the Elder Argent that Kieran was powerful—possibly the most powerful Walker in existence.

Maybe Dakota didn't need to know anything more about Kieran's family because that wasn't what they were any longer.

It was the man who held the door to the conference room open for her who was Kieran's real family. Kieran's brother. Not by blood, but by choice. She smiled at Jackson as she passed. No, she didn't need to know more about the Argents. Kieran had taken the last name Smith to cut all ties. She loved Kieran Smith. Kieran Argent didn't exist any longer.

"There you are," Kieran greeted as she stepped into the room. He was by her side in an instant, taking the drink carrier from her and placing it on the table.

"What's wrong?" Dakota murmured as she found herself wrapped in Kieran's arms.

"I was worried," Kieran whispered. "I don't like you being out of my sight."

She pulled back enough to peer up at her lover. "You know I'm safe here. Plus, Jackson was with me. There's no way your father's going to get close to us here." Dakota believed that to be true one hundred percent. The Elder Argent would be crazy to try to get to them inside the casino.

"Doesn't mean I have to like it when I can't see you," Kieran said. He glared at Jackson. "What'd you do?"

Jackson shrugged. "Picked up coffee. It is a god-awful hour after all."

Kieran straightened as he released Dakota.

"We don't have time for this," Jackson stated. He passed out coffees.

Dakota turned to take in the others in the room. Remy sat next to Kayla with James to his right. The two security guards were stationed behind Kayla, at attention.

Alex helped Jackson get everyone settled. The security guards were dismissed before Dakota took her seat.

"I called Caspar," Remy told her. He eyed Kayla then looked at her. "Sorry but I had to. He's aware of our guest and will make sure she is escorted home."

Dakota couldn't blame Remy for following protocol. Kieran should have done it, and so should she have. "Okay." She turned to her niece. "What do you know about the murder across the street?"

"That's it?" Kayla appeared shocked. "That's what you want to know?"

"Yes." Dakota met Kayla's gaze without flinching. The girl's disbelief and anger grew.

"How about you ask about our family? Your parents? Siblings? Don't you care how any of us are doing?" Kayla shouted.

Dakota wouldn't feel bad. The pain she held inside was for her to deal with.

Kieran growled, but Dakota stroked his leg to keep him calm.

"You were at the scene of the crime hours after we found the body of a young man," Dakota said to Kayla. "Unless you want to be treated as a suspect and have this conversation in much less comfortable surroundings, then you will answer my questions."

"Aren't I supposed to have a lawyer or something?" Kayla smirked.

Beside her Kieran stiffened and Dakota needed to get control of the situation before he lost his temper. She leaned toward her niece while allowing the jaguar close to the surface. Her animal was much stronger than this teenage girl.

"We don't necessarily work within the confines of the law," Dakota growled out. "You know, being a secret Organization and all. You shouldn't even know about us. Unless you want to see a couple of angry Walkers, I suggest you drop the attitude."

Kayla slumped. "I shouldn't have come here."

Well, at least they could agree on something.

"What do you know?" Dakota demanded.

"Okay." Kayla held up her hands. "I really did just come to see you. I lied to my parents and a few of my friends and I drove here. On our first night, we met a couple of guys on the Strip. They were older and bought us drinks. I was still trying to figure out how to approach you. We were going to stay in a cheap motel off the Strip, so it seemed like a good idea when the guys offered us their place to crash."

Dakota nodded to encourage Kayla to continue talking. As she listened, she sipped her coffee. It really was a good brew and she drank deeper.

"When we got to the house, there were all these posters and paint on the walls," Kayla said. "I knew they were satanic symbols, but my friends wanted to stay. They just laughed it off and started to drink more."

"Are your friends shifter or human?" James asked.

"Human," Kayla answered. "They have no idea what I am."

"Did these guys hurt you?" Dakota questioned.

"No." Kayla shook her head. "They were more interested in partying. Drinks, drugs and all that. I just sat back and watched them. At one point, one of the guys, Greg, got a phone call and went into the bedroom."

"You listened in," Dakota guessed.

"Well." Kayla shrugged. "I didn't have anything else to do. I can't get drunk like my friends."

It would be hard, being the only shifter in a world of humans. Having to keep secrets when Kayla knew she was different. Dakota had never had to deal with that though. Once she'd been picked up from her home, she'd trained with other Organization children. The humans had been in awe of the shifters.

"What did you overhear?" Dakota asked.

"It didn't really make sense. Some guy was giving instructions to Greg about something I didn't understand. Greg got real excited talking to the guy. He said the money was almost gone and they needed more."

"Okay," Dakota said. "What else?"

"Nothing much happened after that. My friends and I played tourists and hung out. I watched you, finally approached Kieran and thought the guys were just weird. I mean they play Dungeons and Dragons and go to Comic-Cons. I didn't think they were a danger."

"But something changed your mind?" Dakota pressed.

"Yeah, I followed them to that apartment. They'd talked Carrie and Susie into joining them to party there but hadn't asked me. Said they didn't think I'd be into it. I got concerned. They're my friends. I knew they liked the guys, but I was getting a bad feeling."

Remy got up and grabbed a bottle of water from the center of the table. He cracked open the lid then returned and gave it to Kayla. "Just calmly tell us what happened. It's okay."

"It was nothing," Kayla said. "It sounded like they were tearing up the place and partying. I figured they just wanted a place to hang out. Maybe away from their house in case the cops were called. I came over here and walked around but didn't see with you or Kieran." Kayla glanced at Kieran. "I was hoping Kieran had told you about me."

Dakota didn't respond. At that point she hadn't known about Kayla.

"So anyway, I was back at the coffee shop when I saw you and Kieran leave. I thought I could follow you, but one of the security guards stopped and asked me if I was staying here. That he'd seen me for a few days and reminded me that I was too young to be in the casino section of the hotel. I played along, like I was just getting a coffee and was bored while my parents gambled. When I got outside, you both were gone. I hung around for a little bit then decided to head back to the house. I was going to tell Carrie and Susie that we needed to find a new place to stay. Then I saw all the cops. In the same apartment that my friends were partying at. So I walked over."

"That's when I saw you?" Dakota questioned.

"Not really. I actually hung around the crowd for a while. Someone said there was a dead body. I figured it was an overdose or something. I was scared it was Carrie or Susie. I started to call my friends and Carrie answered and told me that her and Susie were fine. That's when you stepped out of the apartment.

"I was thrilled. I thought I was finally going to meet you," Kayla continued. "You looked over the crowd and your gaze passed right over me. You didn't know who I was."

Dakota shook her head.

"I decided to fuck with you. I thought Kieran hadn't told you or you didn't care."

"We chased you and you ran," Dakota said.

"That was fun," Kayla responded. "I haven't gotten to shift since I left home."

"Where'd you go after that? Where have you been?" Dakota questioned.

"I got back to the house and everyone was asleep. I showered then took a nap myself. I figured when I woke, I'd talk Carrie and Susie into leaving with me."

"They didn't want to leave?" Dakota asked.

"Greg wouldn't let them. He said they were part of his Pack now and they were staying," Kayla told her. "I know they're human, but he said he had the power to make them all live forever. That he'd chosen them. Then he asked if I wanted in. Said I could stay too, but I would have to prove my worth. That Carrie and Susie already passed his test."

Dakota felt sick. Greg's test had no doubt been the murder of the young man.

"I yelled at him and told him he couldn't hold them there. That I'd tell their family where they were, but Greg just laughed. He said he wasn't afraid of human parents. Not when he had the power of the devil. He was crazy!"

"How'd you get away?" James asked.

Dakota was glad he'd picked up the questioning, because Dakota was struggling. She might not approve of what Kayla had done or why she'd come to town, but the teenager's fear was very much real. Dakota could taste on her tongue how badly shaken Kayla was.

"Greg said I'd understand soon and locked me in one of the bedrooms with Carrie and Susie. Susie was acting strange. Like out of it or something. Almost zombie-like."

"What about Carrie?" James pressed.

"She started to go hysterical," Kayla replied. "She actually told me that they'd killed a guy. Picked him up at some café by the university and asked if he wanted to party. Gave him the apartment address. My friends are the ones who picked him out, said he was really good-looking."

Dakota would have to say that their victim hadn't been good-looking when he'd been found.

"Carrie swears she didn't know they were going to kill anyone. They dropped some acid and drank, then Greg said it was time to get started." Kayla shuddered. "I can't—I can't repeat what she said."

"You don't have to," James said. "Not right now. What I do need is for you to tell me where the house is and the names of everyone involved." He pulled out a notebook and pen from his pocket and set them in front of Kayla.

"You'll help them though, right?" Kayla turned in her chair toward Dakota. "You have to help my friends."

"Right now, we're more worried about getting your friends out alive," Dakota told her. "With them doing such heavy drugs, there's a good chance someone else is going to get hurt soon. We need to get your friends out."

"Okay." Kayla grasped Dakota's hand. "Just…just watch out for them. This is all my fault."

Dakota pressed her lips together then nodded. She glanced over at Kieran. "I'll meet you guys upstairs. Let me have a minute alone with Kayla."

"No," Kieran said. "Everyone else can go, but I stay."

She rolled her eyes. *Like something's going to happen to me in the few floors that separate Jackson's office from ours.*

"Write down the address and names," Dakota told Kayla.

The teenager scribbled the information down and slid it over to James. James and Remy stood then headed for the door.

"We'll give you some privacy," Jackson said. "Then keep an eye on the girl until Caspar gets here."

Dakota nodded. She waited until it was only her, Kieran and Kayla in the room before turning to her niece. "I know you wanted to talk to me, but you shouldn't have come."

"I know that," Kayla replied. "I just wanted to know more about you."

"But you can't," Dakota told her gently. "There are rules in place for a reason. I'm not your aunt. I'm an agent for the Organization. That's all I am. I can't be more to you. I'll never be the aunt you're looking for."

Kayla shook her head and her shoulders dropped. "It's not fair."

Dakota rose. She laid her hand on the girl's shoulder. "Life is hardly fair. And I'm sorry I can't give you the answers you want. But, Kayla?"

"Yeah?" The teenager looked rejected and sad.

"If things were different, I would like to get to know you," Dakota said. She even meant it. "You're pretty cool and I'm proud of you."

Kayla looked up at her. "Really?"

"It took a lot of courage to come to find me. I'm sorry you got mixed up in all this. You should talk to your parents, though. Let them help you."

"I will," Kayla promised. "I miss them."

"Bye, Kayla." She squeezed one last time then walked away. Dakota didn't figure she'd see her niece again.

Jackson and Alex stood outside the door.

"Everything okay?" Jackson asked.

"Will you keep an eye on her for me?" Dakota asked.

"Yes. I already ordered her some food," Jackson responded. "If she needs some rest, I'll get a her in a room."

"Let her call her parents?" Dakota requested. "Caspar won't like it but—"

"I'll take care of it," Jackson promised.

"Thanks." She walked toward the elevator with Kieran by her side.

"You lied," he said when they stopped to wait for the elevator doors.

"What?" Dakota didn't lie.

"That's not all you are," he said.

"What else?" she asked. God, she was fucking tired.

"You're also my mate," Kieran responded. He pulled her close then pushed her face into his neck.

His scent, the familiar smell, grounded her. "Thanks."

Chapter Eight

They decided to hit the house as soon as possible. With the alcohol and drugs being so heavily used, Greg and his friends were still passed out.

Kieran was impressed that Dakota had put such a solid plan in place and had all the agents organized a block from the house. He wanted to keep her inside the hotel where she was safe and his father couldn't touch her. Dakota wasn't the type of agent to allow others to go in her place, though. She insisted on going in and leading from the field. She'd made Kayla a promise to watch out for the girl's friends so no matter how much Kieran argued, Dakota was heading the op.

It both frustrated and turned him on how strong she was.

That was something that his father would never be able to take away — Dakota's strength. And because she was strong, Kieran's father wasn't going to win.

"You listening to me?" Dakota waved her hand in front of his face.

"Of course," he lied.

She snorted. "I want you to grab Greg. I want to know who this man is that he's talking to. This isn't over until we get whoever is pulling the strings."

"Sure, no problem." Kieran looked around at all the other agents and Damon's Pack members. Dakota had called in the Alpha and invited him to join them as a sort of apology. Damon hadn't hesitated in coming with two Enforcers. "Do you really think all this is necessary? From the way Kayla spoke, they're just humans."

Dakota grabbed his arm and dragged him away from the others. "I don't want anyone underestimating these guys," she hissed. "You remember what they did to that poor young man? They might have someone pulling their strings, but they did that. They tortured and killed a poor college student who hadn't done anything wrong."

"You're right." Kieran gripped both her shoulders. "I'll be careful and you do the same."

"Thank you." She rose and kissed him quickly. "Besides, remember that as soon as we finish this, I'm claiming you. I want my bite to be the only new mark on that fabulous body of yours."

In an instant he was rock-hard and Kieran groaned. "That wasn't nice at all."

She smirked. "Later, lover."

It took every ounce of control he had to allow her to skip away laughing. Kieran wanted to pull her into the closest alley and ravage her. Damn it, he needed to focus. He thumped his cock, hoping to relieve some pressure.

"That had to hurt."

He growled at James and the human grinned.

"Trouble with your girlfriend?" James teased.

"Careful there, James," Kieran responded. "Both my girlfriend and I have really sharp teeth."

James laughed, but another powerful rumble sounded behind him. Kieran turned as Damon stalked toward him.

"Did you just threaten him?" Damon demanded, stepping right into Kieran's personal space.

Kieran straightened and tried to hide his amusement.

"Jesus Christ," James muttered. He stepped in between Kieran and Damon. "Everything is fine, Alpha. Why don't you go growl at someone else?" He patted Damon's chest but then began to caress it. He hummed low.

Kieran rolled his eyes. Those two needed to fuck and get it over with. He cleared his throat. "Should I give you two a few minutes alone? I'm sure I could cover for you. It shouldn't take that long to blow your load."

James jerked like he'd been shocked. "Asshole." He stomped off as Kieran chuckled.

"You are an asshole," Damon said with a glare. "Was that really necessary?"

"Hey, it's not my fault you can't get your head out of your ass and pound that boy like he obviously wants."

"Not all of us are ruled by our cocks," Damon responded. "Just don't threaten him again." Damon followed behind James.

"Those two are going to tear each other apart once they get it on," Remy stated as he joined Kieran.

"Right!" Kieran exclaimed.

"Twenty-four hours," Remy said.

"What in twenty-four hours?"

"That they're fucking," Remy replied.

"No way." Kieran glanced over to where Damon was hovering behind James as the human agent tried to ignore him. "Damon's too stubborn. It will take him at least forty-eight hours."

"Hundred bucks?" Remy held out his hand.

"Hundred bucks." Kieran slapped his palm.

"I don't want to know what you're betting on," Dakota said, coming up to his side. "We're ready."

"You really don't," Kieran agreed. "I'm riding with you."

Dakota whistled sharply. "Let's go."

Dakota drove with Kieran by her side and Remy, James and Damon in the back seat. The human situated between the two shifters bitched about Damon not going with his Enforcers. Damon ignored James, but Kieran knew that the Alpha was ensuring James' safety. Kieran would have done the same. Damn it, he might lose the bet.

The other SUVs followed behind close to Dakota's bumper. More were headed to the house from the opposite direction. They would roll right up to the front door then storm the place. Dakota hadn't wanted to give their suspects time to think.

Three houses from their target, Dakota removed her seatbelt. "Get ready," she ordered.

Kieran already had his fingers on the door handle.

She gunned the engine, making the SUV hop the curb before she drove through the yard. Dakota slammed on the brakes right before she would have hit the front steps. "Move!" she shouted.

Kieran pushed open his door and flew to the front door with Damon close at his heels. He lifted his foot and slammed it into the side of the door. The wood splintered and he pushed the rest of the entrance out of the way. Sometimes his enhanced strength really helped.

"Go right," he told Damon, seeing all the doors closed.

He started left when he heard a familiar sound. "Fuck!" He turned, knocking James off his feet then tackling Dakota.

The shotgun blast tore at the closest door.

Kieran lifted his head to check on the other agents. Remy had followed Damon and both wolf shifters had dropped to the ground. Dakota cursed under him while James groaned.

Anger swamped him. Kieran jumped to his feet and was across the room, slamming the door open before another shot could go off.

Inside the room, a naked man sat up in bed holding a shotgun while a young woman huddled in the corner. He recognized Greg and Carrie from the pictures Mitch had printed of all their suspects.

Kieran strode forward as Greg got another shot off. Kieran dodged out of the way, letting the bullets go over his shoulder before he grabbed the weapon with one hand and Greg's throat with the other.

He lifted the naked human off the bed as he flashed his fangs.

"What the fuck are you?" Greg screamed.

Kieran shook the pathetic excuse for a man.

"Don't kill him," Dakota called out.

He turned. "You okay?"

"Fine." She spotted Carrie cowering and walked to her. "Hey, Carrie, it's okay."

"What...what's going on? What is he?" She lifted a trembling finger and pointed it at Kieran.

"It doesn't matter." Dakota crouched down in front of the teenager. "We're here to help."

Kieran turned his attention back to Greg. "You're coming with me."

Urine assaulted his senses as Greg pissed himself.

"Damn it." Kieran really wanted to strangle the loser now. He had no trouble torturing and killing an innocent college student, but when confronted, he'd peed himself? These were not the type of people Kieran suspected would be involved in ritual killings. It was kind of disappointing.

"Please don't kill me!" Greg begged.

Dakota led Carrie out of the room with a blanket wrapped around her, so Kieran moved in close to Greg.

"Is that what the poor kid you tortured and killed said? Did he beg for his life? Ask why you were hurting him?"

Greg's eyes widened. "What? How?"

"What the fuck do you think we're doing here, Greg?" Kieran spat. "You killed someone and now it's time to pay."

"No! He said I would be safe. No one would know who I was. He'd protect me!" Greg babbled.

"Who?" Kieran demanded. "The only way to save yourself is to tell me who is behind this." Kieran showed Greg his fangs once again.

"Fu...fuck yooooou," Greg howled. "He'll kill me."

"I'll kill you!" Kieran roared. He let the full Walker out and to the surface, the glowing blue eyes and full-length fangs.

"*Nooooooo!*" Greg screamed.

Kieran yanked Greg close and clamped his fangs down on Greg's shoulder. He wanted to make the little human suffer and a few sips would both strengthen Kieran and make Greg sick.

"I don't know his name, I swear. He came to me one night and told me he could make me immortal. Gave me money. A lot of money. I'll talk!" Greg promised.

Kieran withdrew his fangs, satisfied. Greg didn't know that the small amount that Kieran had taken was all he needed. "Your blood tastes good. Maybe I'll want more if you stop talking."

"Help me! He's going to eat me!"

"I didn't see anything," Dakota said, striding forward. "No one will. Maybe I should let him tear your throat out. Fitting, don't you think?"

"My phone!" Greg was crying now. "He calls me. I have his number."

Dakota walked over to the bedside table and picked up a new iPhone. She pressed the Home button then grunted.

"What?" Kieran asked.

"Moron didn't even password protect it," she commented. "Let's take him in."

Greg groaned. "Oh God! I'm going to be sick. What'd you do to me?"

Ah, the side effects of being bitten by the Walker.

"I'll take him outside before he starts puking," Kieran said. "I love this part."

"Everyone else has been rounded up. Both girls are headed to the hospital. I want them looked at. They were still in shock."

"Okay, let's get him in a call and talking," Kieran grinned at Greg. "Or I might get hungry again."

"No, no, please. I'll cooperate."

Piece of shit. That was all Kieran could think as he literally dragged Greg outside.

"You're gonna owe me a hundred bucks," Remy cackled as Kieran stepped onto the porch.

"What?"

Remy nodded toward the SUV. Damon had James pinned, rutting against him and sniffing his neck. James, his legs around the Alpha's waist and his head back, was encouraging the Alpha.

"Shit, what'd I miss?"

"Seems that shot you knocked James out of the way of infuriated our Alpha. After he punched out the human males, he threw James over his shoulder and they've been like that ever since."

Kieran chuckled. "Gotta love those Alpha hormones."

"I'm pretty sure they're going to be fucking any moment. No one wants to be the one to break them up."

"I'll do it," Kieran grumbled. He wasn't afraid of Damon, but an Alpha desperate to mate was a little more than he could handle alone. He thumped down the steps, letting Greg feel each one.

Greg was struggling and crying, but Kieran found him easy to ignore.

"Hey, Alpha!" Kieran called. "If you step away from the agent, I'll give you one shot at this one." He dangled Greg in the air.

Damon lifted his head and growled. His wolf was so close to the surface his hands had shifted into claws.

"No!" Greg yelled.

The agents around the yard all paused to see what was going on.

Damon gently placed James with his feet back on the ground then kissed his forehead. James sighed and nuzzled him before straightening his clothes. His lips were puffy and there was definite beard burn on his neck.

"Claws in," Kieran ordered as Damon stalked forward. "I promised Dakota he wouldn't die. Yet. We need answers first."

The Alpha nodded and flexed his fingers that were normal again.

"You tried to kill my mate." Damon sounded as though he'd swallowed glass.

A shiver went through Kieran at the ultimate display of power from the Alpha. Kieran had never met anyone who had such strength. Still not more than Kieran, but Damon was one hell of a shifter.

"I...what...no..."

Damon pulled back and punched Greg in the face. Kieran released the human, so he would fly back and not break his neck.

Greg hit the side of the house just as Dakota stepped out of the house.

"What the hell in going on out here?" she yelled.

All the agents who had been watching scurried to look busy. She looked at Remy who hadn't moved from leaning against the wall.

Remy shrugged. "Must have closed my eyes. I didn't get a lot of sleep last night."

Dakota leaned down and yanked Greg's head back. She sniffed then turned toward them. "Really, Damon? You're here as a consultant."

"I consulted," Damon responded smoothly. "With my fist."

"Children. I'm surrounded by children," Dakota muttered.

Kieran slapped Damon on the back. "Let's get this done so we can all go home."

Damon turned to James. "Yeah, I have plans tonight."

James blushed then opened the back door. He muttered something about pushy Alphas as Kieran and Damon shared a grin. It was turning out to be a pretty good day. And if Kieran and Damon would scare Greg into confessing all his sins, they might be done by dinner time.

* * * *

Three a.m., the witching hour, and the time that Dakota let herself and Kieran back into their suite. She'd been awake for over twenty-four hours and had heard more supernatural lore and ridiculous stories than she ever wanted to. That was why she was thinking about witches, demons and vampires as she kicked off her shoes.

"That was interesting," Kieran commented.

"It was an utter waste of time," Dakota corrected. "He doesn't even know who he was talking to. Just some guy who gave him money and convinced him he'd become immortal. Without any proof. That kid, the one from UNLV, died for no reason."

"We'll find out who's behind all this," Kieran promised.

She knew they'd try, but the number that had been contacting Greg was already disconnected and they'd traced it to a burner phone. No other information had been available. It was a dead end. They'd questioned every member of Greg's group but had only heard tales of the supernatural and how they were going to rule the world. The fact that none of them had known they were dealing with the real supernatural was a laughing matter. If she wasn't so damn tired...

"Hey." Kieran wrapped his arms around her and nuzzled her neck. "It was a tough case, but we stopped anyone else from getting hurt. The girls are headed back home with their families. The humans will serve time for murder. We have to call this a win."

Dakota threaded her fingers through Kieran's where they rested against her stomach. Caspar had given her permission to continue working the case and keep an eye out for their main suspect. With the number being disconnected, there was a good chance their main suspect was already on the run. But that didn't mean he'd give up, though. Whatever the ultimate goal was, he'd probably try again. And Dakota would get closer next time. "You know what this means?"

Kieran kissed her neck. "I already made plans for us to have the weekend off." He turned her. "I want you to claim me."

She nodded. Dakota wanted that so badly. "Not tonight, though."

He frowned. "Why not?"

"Because I want it to be perfect. Not after being awake for an entire day, chasing bad guys and having all these images in my head of the murder scene. I want to do it. Soon. Just not tonight."

"I get it," he whispered. "What can I do for you right now then? Shower? Food? Sleep?"

Dakota shook her head. "I need you." She kissed his chin. His cheek. "Help me clear my head?"

"Oh, I can do that." Kieran picked her up then walked over to the window. "And I know how much my girl loves her kinky side."

She shuddered. The window. God, she loved when Kieran took her against the window. The special windows ensured that no one could see in, but Dakota loved the thought of being watched as Kieran owned her body.

"Hands on the glass," he ordered.

Dakota placed her palms on the cool window. Below her, hundreds of tourists strolled down the street, having no idea that high above them two people were making love.

"You're so beautiful," he purred against her neck. "I love how strong you are."

He pulled her shirt and sports bra over her head, causing her to move her hands. But she quickly returned her palms back where he'd said so he wouldn't stop, or take her in the bedroom.

This was exactly what she needed.

The city alive below her and she had private time with her lover. Her mate.

Kieran kissed down her back; causing goosebumps to break out. He even used his sharp fangs down the small of her back, although he didn't draw blood.

"Yes," she hissed, allowing her head to fall back.

He cupped her breasts then thumbed her nipples. She fucking loved his hands. The way that he worshipped her body.

Kieran slipped his hands down her stomach to the button of her black utility pants. He snapped it open then pulled the zipper down.

"Boots," she said, wiggling her foot.

He laughed but untied her boots and removed them, along with her socks.

Dakota shimmied her hips, making her pants fall a few inches.

"Fuck, I love you," Kieran murmured. He kissed the back of her ear then sucked the lobe into his mouth.

"Mmm." She arched, pressing her boobs against the glass and her ass against his hard cock.

He pushed the pants down the hips and legs, leaving her only a pair of cotton boy shorts. Kieran brushed his finger over the front of her crotch where she was already wet. She needed him inside her. Dakota rocked so she rubbed his erection into her ass.

"So needy," he teased, slipping his finger under the elastic of her panties.

"Please," she begged. "Please."

Entering one thick digit inside her, Kieran thrust his hips at the same time.

"Kieran," she said. "Not enough."

"Turn your head," he demanded. "Kiss me."

That was one order she had no problem following. Dakota kissed him with every ounce of love she felt, even letting her jaguar close to the surface so the animal felt how much their mate cared and appreciated them.

"My clothes on or off?" he asked, adding a second digit.

"On. Please on." She dropped her head back to his chest.

"My naughty girl," he murmured. Then ripped off her panties and let them flutter to the floor.

Dakota plastered herself against the window, watching the reflection as Kieran struggled with the button of his pants.

Getting his cock out, Kieran gripped her hips. "I want to hear you. Don't hold back."

He entered her slowly and that was not what she wanted. Dakota threw herself back until she impaled on his straining shaft.

Drawing his hand back, Kieran slapped her ass. "Bad girl."

Dakota laughed in delight.

He spanked her again.

"Yes! Yes!" she encouraged.

A third swat came then Kieran began to move. He plunged his cock over and over, faster and harder, until she was indeed screaming his name.

There was nothing like the feel of Kieran owning every inch of her.

He drove in and she could only brace herself against the window. When she was with Kieran like this, she didn't have to think of anything else. Not her job, friends, the family that didn't care about her. All Dakota needed to know was that Kieran loved her and he was desperate to claim her. Much the same way that she would one day soon claim him.

Her body bounced in response to his urgent thrusts, Kieran's grip on her waist tight enough to bruise. He slammed into her with an animalist hunger. This was what connected them.

Kieran could read her, knew what she craved.

"More," she yelled.

He was on the verge of losing control and she was the only one who could handle him.

Dakota laid her cheek against the cold glass and closed her eyes as she drifted into the warm safe place that Kieran was driving her to.

She cried out her pleasure as the orgasm was ripped from her body.

Kieran didn't stop, though. He continued to plunder her until he held her up.

"Love you," he grunted out then came.

His hot seed filled her and she was complete for the first time all day. Kieran murmured sweet nothings to her while kissing her neck, shoulders and back.

The sharp insistent ring of her cell phone pulled her from contentment.

"No," she cried. "It can't be ringing. We have the weekend off."

Kieran grunted. "This is fucking ridiculous. Who the fuck is calling you?"

"I don't know as you have me pinned to the window with your magnificent cock still inside me," Dakota teased.

Her cell stopped ringing.

"Good. I wanted round two."

The phone rang again.

"Damn it." Kieran gently pulled out then bent and picked up her pants.

Dakota dug through the pockets until she had the annoying device in her hand. Jackson's name was on the screen.

"Hello?"

"Six-twelve Ashcott Drive. I have him. Get here now or it'll be over," Jackson said before he hung up.

Dakota looked up at her lover.

"What was that about?"

"Okay," she said, cupping his face. "Don't be mad."

Chapter Nine

Don't be mad. Those were the words that the woman he loved more than anything else in the world said before she confessed Jackson's plan to capture and kill his father. Kieran didn't know whether to laugh or strangle Dakota as she drove them to the address that Jackson had given her.

For a moment he'd actually thought that Dakota was going to try to talk him out of going with her. She'd opened her mouth then closed it before shaking her head. With a comment that they needed to get dressed and hurry before Jackson lost his patience, she hadn't said another word.

There were no street lights on this side of town. They'd been driving for twenty minutes before she started to slow the SUV down. She turned into a driveway of a rundown house with boarded-up windows.

Dakota stopped and put the vehicle in park then sat there staring up at the front door.

Kieran gave her the time she seemed to need.

"We don't have to go inside," she whispered. "I could just put the vehicle in reverse and drive away. Hell, we don't even have to go back to the hotel. We could just drive."

Kieran wasn't surprised she was having doubts. The goodness inside Dakota was one of the reasons he loved her so much. But Kieran couldn't walk away. Not from this.

"No one even has to know we were ever here," she said. "We could just drive away."

He nodded. "We could."

"We're not going to, are we?"

"You can stay in the car," he offered.

Dakota sighed but turned the ignition off. "Make me a promise?"

"Anything," he vowed.

"No matter what that man says, remember who you are," she demanded.

"I promise."

"Kieran," she said, turning in her seat. "Kieran Smith, my mate, Remy's partner, Jackson's best friend, Caspar's son. You remember who you are."

Kieran closed his eyes. The first time he'd seen Caspar, the human had walked through smoke into the room where Kieran's cell had been. He'd crouched down in front of Kieran and smiled. Then he'd asked if Kieran was ready to get the hell out of there. Jackson was there in his memories. The time that they'd held hands through the bars as Kieran had struggled to breath with four broken ribs. The first time he'd met Remy. The wolf shifter had stood toe to toe with Kieran, glaring at being called a lap dog. Kieran still enjoyed needling his partner. And Dakota, standing in that dark alley, over the unconscious bodies of the men Kieran had beaten up. There'd been something in the way that she'd had her feet braced apart, hands on hips, glaring, that had shown him his life would never be the same.

But there were more people than just those four. Alex, Jackson's right-hand man, a good Walker and a friend to Kieran. Damon, the asshole Alpha, who'd helped both him and Dakota more times than he should have. Mitch, the young Walker, who looked up to Kieran and helped with his hijinks. Charlie, the front guard who was growing into a capable agent. James, the human who would be a real asset to the Organization. Angel, his old partner and the mutt she'd mated with.

All those people had made an impression on Kieran, had helped mold him into the person he was. His father couldn't touch those memories, no matter how much hate he spewed. "I swear to you that I will remember who I am."

Dakota nodded, although she didn't look any less worried.

The front door opened and Alex stepped out. He wore jeans and nothing else. He had a rag in his hand as he wiped what looked like blood from his chest.

"I guess we should see if he's already dead," Dakota murmured.

Kieran pushed his door open then walked to the front of the SUV. He waited until Dakota slipped her hand in his before he took a step forward.

Alex walked down the steps to meet them. "You don't have to go inside. Jackson and I can handle this."

"Is he dead?" Kieran asked. It was hard to get the words out.

"No, we were just having a little fun as we waited on you."

"Then I'm going in," Kieran said.

Lights flashed over them. Kieran swung around, placing Dakota behind him. Alex stepped up to his side.

"Uh, guys," Dakota grumbled. "Trained agent here."

Kieran didn't respond though. He watched the two vehicles pull up and park behind Dakota's SUV.

"Is that Caspar?" Alex growled. "Damn it."

"How in the hell?" Kieran asked. Not only had Caspar and Remy just arrived, but Damon and James were climbing out of the other vehicle.

Dakota pushed through Kieran's and Alex's shoulders. "What are you guys doing here?"

"I called them."

Kieran turned to Jackson, where he stood at the threshold of the house. "Why?"

"Your father has information that your Organization needs to know," Jackson told him.

"But—" If Caspar took custody of his father, he wouldn't be killed.

"We made a deal," Jackson told him. He nodded at Caspar. "It didn't take much convincing to get your boss to agree to allowing me to keep your father after he's been questioned."

Kieran didn't understand. He glanced at his boss. The man who had been there for him when he'd had no one else. Caspar had seen him through the darkest days Kieran had suffered through after his rescue.

"I know more than anyone what evil lives inside that man," Caspar said, gripping his shoulder.

"What is everyone else doing here?" he questioned.

"We're here for you, buddy," Remy said.

"Great," Kieran snapped. "We should have ordered a pizza."

"Funny," Jackson commented. "Can we take this inside before one of the neighbors gets curious?"

"Yes," Caspar responded. "We need to."

Kieran let everyone else walk up the stairs except for him and Dakota. He'd gotten a back slap from Damon and a smile from James. Now he stood staring at the entrance of the house, grasping Dakota's hand, needing her strength.

"We can still leave," she told him. "No one will blame you."

"Tell me I'm strong enough to do this," he requested. Kieran felt like that lost boy whose his father had first sent him away, unsure what do to and where to go.

"You are strong enough," Dakota stated firmly. She placed her hand over his heart. "Because of who you are, not where you came from. That man in there might have donated the seed that gave you life, but he doesn't get to claim one delicious inch of you, and especially not your heart. That belongs to me."

He yanked her forward then laid his mouth over hers. He slipped his tongue inside when she opened up for him. When he pulled back, he was grinning. "This really is the last obstacle in your claiming of me. I want it to happen tonight. In our room. We could go away and stay somewhere else, but I really want to start our mated life together in the bed we share."

"That sounds perfect to me," she agreed, her palm against his cheek.

"Tonight," he said.

"Tonight," she repeated.

He wrapped his arm around her shoulder then led her up the four steps. The old rotted porch threatened to collapse under their feet.

"I wonder where Jackson found this place," Dakota commented.

"I think it's better we don't know," Kieran replied.

"The house is scheduled to be torn down next week. Jackson is having a community center in its place. The center will offer after-school programs for the kids, night education for parents and free meals to whoever needs them," Alex said as they entered.

"Stop listening into our conversations," Kieran grumbled.

Alex grinned. "So Mitch was removing all the electronics we used during your investigation in the suite next to yours earlier tonight…"

"Oh, God." Dakota leaned her forehead against his shoulder.

"I believe he said that phrase was yelled—"

"Shut it," Kieran warned with a growl.

Alex merely beamed back.

"I changed my mind," Kieran told him. "I hate you."

"Sure, brother," Alex said. "Sure." He waved them forward. "The others are already inside the bedroom, waiting."

Kieran straightened his shoulders then strode across the room and down the hall. No one was talking, cursing or making threats as he paused in the doorway.

His father was in a chair with his hands, ankles and waist wrapped in rope holding him secure. But it wasn't the man he remembered from his nightmares. His father had aged, and not well, which surprised Kieran. Walkers were immortal—they could live forever if they chose to. His father wouldn't be showing such signs unless be was abusing his power or playing with black magic.

"That's him?" Dakota murmured. "Not what I expected."

"Yeah, me neither," Kieran responded.

His father lifted his head and sneered. "There is nothing wrong with my hearing, boy. Now get over here and untie me."

Kieran wanted to laugh. He felt no fear from the man in front of him. It had nothing to do with the dry blood, bruises or wounds on his father. No, Kieran could feel his power, so his father still held some strength. But he was weak compared to him. Hell, even Jackson and Damian held more ability than his father. "Why would I do that?" He walked with calm, even steps across the room to stand before the man who'd haunted him.

"Because I am your father. Look at these people in the room. They're not your family. I am." Then he turned his head and lifted his lip at Dakota. "I'll even allow you to keep your pet. As long as you leash her."

Dakota stomped forward, but Kieran held up his hand. She stopped.

Kieran's father laughed. "Maybe you already have a leash on her."

Dakota was growling but didn't move.

"No, I have what's called respect. Hers and those in this room. But you wouldn't know anything about that, would you?" He crouched so he was even with his father. "You rule with fear and pain."

"I rule," his father responded. "And you all will pay for this."

Kieran shook his head. "Can't you see its over? You're finished."

"Am I?" he laughed. "You think one of your little cells will hold me? Me, the Elder of the most powerful clan of Walkers?"

Jackson strode forward. "Why don't you tell them what you told me? About your distraction."

"Distraction?" Kieran asked.

"The man behind the ritual killings," Jackson supplied.

Dakota gasped as Caspar joined them in a circle around his father.

"You?" Caspar questioned.

"I wanted to see how your little group worked," his dad said. "It was fun. Watching you all chase your tails. Fitting for a group of animals."

Jackson strode behind his father and yanked his head back. "Not all of us."

"No." His father clenched his teeth. "But you have your own weakness, don't you, Jackson Wickham? You think you can take care of so many people. That they appreciate it. They're using you."

Jackson allowed his fangs to drop. "It must be hard to live in a world where you have to watch your back twenty-four-seven. When you can't trust anyone."

"Trust?" his father spat. "What would you know about trust?"

Kieran smiled. "Everything." He looked over at Dakota then waved her forward. "Is there anything you want to say?"

Dakota leaned down to hover in front of his father's face. "He doesn't belong to you. He never did. Kieran is the most powerful Walker in existence and it had nothing to do with you. You'll have no legacy when you die. No one will mourn you. Because you are nothing." Then she drew back her hand and backslapped him. Just once. "That's for hurting my mate."

"Mate?" his father roared. "You can't mate with him! He will follow my orders. Kieran, untie me now."

The rush of power that assaulted him barely even registered. Not only to him but everyone in the room. James sneezed then rubbed his nose.

"What was that?" James asked.

"A pathetic attempt to use what little power the Elder of the most powerful Walker clan has," Damon responded. "A new-born pup could probably make you sneeze, my mate."

"Wait," Dakota turned. Her back was to his father, the ultimate insult. "You mated?"

James blushed but nodded. "Uh, yeah. Earlier tonight."

"Congratulations!" Dakota exclaimed.

This time when his father pushed his power, Kieran felt it, but it was almost a tickle.

James laughed, Remy groaned and Kieran was shocked. His father slumped with sweat pouring of his body.

"There's no point in fighting any longer," Kieran advised. "You're too weak and no one is coming to save you."

"I have money," his father responded. "Put me in a cell and I'll be out in less than twenty-four hours. Then I'll be back, and next time, you won't see me coming. I'll destroy this entire city, everyone you care about, then drag you home to your rightful place by my side."

"No," Kieran said. He wasn't sad or upset. The ending of the relationship with his father meant nothing, really. Finding out that he'd used Greg, the teenage girls and an innocent young man sealed his father's fate. He would never stop coming for Kieran, which would put those he cared about in constant danger. "That's not going to happen. No one said anything about arresting you."

His father furrowed his brow.

"You are not leaving this house alive," Kieran said. "Once we have what we want, you. Are. Dead."

"You wouldn't dare kill me. You don't have the nerve."

"Well, Dad." Kieran smirked. "You don't know me now, do you? Or what I would do. But no, I'm not going to kill you. I have something much more important that I need to be doing. Like spending time with the woman that I love."

His father snorted. "Love? What a lie. She'll leave you for one of her own kind."

"No, she won't," Kieran responded. "Because we belong together. I have faith in her."

"Don't you leave me here," his father shouted. "Think about your mother."

"My mother," he repeated. "The woman who ignored me unless it was to hurl insults? That's not going to work on me."

"You'll leave her widowed? Alone in the world?"

"Because being married to you is so much better?" Kieran asked. "Don't worry, though, my mother has always craved more power than what she actually processed. I'm sure she'll have you replaced in no time."

The words must have hit close to the truth because his father really started to struggle to get loose. He cursed, threatened and tried to wiggle out of his bindings until he exhausted himself.

"Fine, leave me, but then you'll never know where I got all my information on you from."

Kieran looked at Jackson who shook his head. Okay, so Jackson hadn't gotten that information yet.

"It'll be easier on you if you just tell us," Kieran tried. "We'll make your death quick."

"Weak, you're still so weak."

Kieran stepped back. He was finished with this man. "He's all yours," he told Caspar.

Caspar smiled at him. "I hear we'll have something to celebrate tomorrow?"

Kieran looked over his shoulder at Alex. He'd been the only one close enough to overhear them.

Alex shrugged. "I was excited for you."

"Yes." He turned back to Caspar. "Tonight."

"I'm happy for you," Caspar told him. "So fucking happy." He embraced Kieran.

"Well, isn't that sweet," his father mocked.

It didn't matter, though. He gripped Caspar tightly for a moment then released him. "You sure you don't need me to stay?"

"We got this," Caspar assured him. "Go and enjoy your mate."

Kieran led Dakota over to where Damon was leaning against the wall with James in his arms. "What exactly are the two of you doing here?" That hadn't really been explained earlier.

Damon stopped nuzzling James' neck for a minute to answer. "Back up. Jackson had a feeling we needed to be here. He couldn't explain it."

"Well, congratulations," he said. Then winked at James. "Even if you cost me a hundred bucks."

"A hundred bucks?" James asked.

Remy hooted. "I told you!"

Kieran pulled out his wallet then slapped Remy's winnings into his partner's hand. "You two couldn't have kept it in your pants for forty-eight hours?"

Damon growled. "You bet on our sex life?"

"Or lack of," Kieran responded.

Damon swiped out, but Kieran danced out of the way.

"I'll see you later?" Kieran asked Remy.

"You supply the beer and I'll bring the pizza," Remy promised.

Kieran punched Remy's shoulder before looking back at his boss. He nodded to Caspar for the interrogation to begin then pulled Dakota along to leave.

"I have some questions for you," Caspar stated.

Kieran took one last look around the room. Caspar stood tall in front of Kieran's father with Alex and Jackson at his back. Kieran was walking away from his father, and he trusted the men in the room to make sure Kieran was finally safe.

"And if I don't want to answer?" he heard his father respond as he stepped out of the room.

"You okay?" Dakota asked.

"Better than okay," he assured her. "It's really over."

"Yes, yes, it is."

Kieran laughed then picked her up and raced to the SUV. "Shit, we're blocked in."

Dakota groaned.

"Hey!" Remy steeped out onto the porch. "Take ours." He tossed the keys to Kieran.

"Thanks, man," Kieran called as Dakota threw her set to Remy.

"Just don't let him drive," Remy replied. "I just got it detailed."

Dakota swiped the keys from him. "I don't have a death wish."

Kieran grumbled but he was too happy to really complain. As he climbed into the passenger seat, Remy disappeared back into the house. Kieran tried to find some sort of compassion for what would happen to his father, but instead he could only remember the many times that he had been punished. His father's punishments had grown more severe as Kieran had aged and too many had been undeserved. There was an entire clan that would be better off when the Elder Argent didn't return.

He kept his hand on Dakota's thigh for the entire drive back to the hotel.

They didn't speak, much like earlier, except this time the sexual tension in the vehicle was overwhelming. Dakota had said she wanted to wait to claim him, but Kieran didn't know if he would be able to. Now that the last link to his old life had been severed, Kieran felt free. He didn't have to worry about his past coming back for them. Instead he could concentrate on the long future they'd have, side by side.

Dakota pulled into the parking garage and into her assigned spot.

"I want you to claim me as soon as we get inside," Kieran told her. "I don't want to wait any longer."

She turned to him. "I'm not sure I could hold back anyway. I want you to be mine and I want everyone to know."

"They will," he vowed.

"I'm shaking," she said

Kieran covered her hand with his. "Me too."

Dakota smiled and he knew that he would spend the rest of his days putting that happiness in her eyes. He pulled her forward to pepper gentle kisses over her chin and up to her mouth. She moaned as their lips met. This was heaven, having the taste of his beloved on his tongue.

Her phone rang and Kieran pulled back with a snarl.

"You've got to be fucking kidding me!" He grabbed her cell from where she was fumbling with it.

"What?" he snapped, having seen Remy's name on the caller ID.

"Your father gave us the name of the agent who's working for him," Remy said.

"Then take care of it!" Kieran yelled. "As of this minute, we have three days off and we're taking them."

"Kieran." Remy's tone was quiet and urgent. "It's Caden."

"What's Caden?" he asked. Who gave a damn about the lion shifter? Kieran hadn't even seen him this last day.

Remy sighed and Kieran's frustration increased. Would he ever get any time with Dakota away from the Organization? It'd been his choice to join the group, but all Kieran wanted was to be inside his suite with the woman he loved.

He started to hang up on Remy, but Dakota plucked the phone out of his hand. She'd had heard both sides of the conversation, but if she thought they were turning around —

"Caden betrayed us?" Dakota asked.

"What?" Kieran questioned. He was so horny and his head was only on thoughts of becoming Dakota's mate.

"Yeah," Remy answered.

Kieran cursed while sinking down in his seat. He took a deep breath and counted to five so he could focus.

"It turns out that Caden's been trying to find a way out of the Organization for years. When Kieran's father offered him enough money to disappear along with the resources to do so, Caden had no problem switching sides," Remy told them.

"I'll gut him," Dakota growled.

Damn, that rumble turned him on. Kieran adjusted his erection into a more comfortable position. He was pretty sure he wasn't going to get laid anytime soon. Not with this new development.

Remy chuckled. "Caspar wants you to keep an eye out and be careful. We've got teams out searching for Caden, but no one has seen him for several hours. Not since Jackson and Alex took Kieran's father. He could be on the run."

"But you don't think so," Dakota relied.

"No, we don't," Remy agreed. "He didn't get the money and we know who he is. Caden is probably going to be desperate."

"And he might come for Kieran," Dakota said. She glanced at him and he shook his head.

Five minutes. If they could have waited five damn minutes, Kieran and Dakota would be up in their suite and none of this would have mattered until they came up for air. Hopefully, in three days.

"What do you want us to do?" Dakota asked.

"Nothing," Remy said. "Just be careful. Alex already let the security at the hotel know. Watch your back and if you spot Caden, call it in."

"You expect us to just let this go?" Dakota demanded. "This was my investigation! He betrayed my team!"

"And you closed your case," Remy told her. "But Caden's actions reflect on all of us. Caspar wants Caden inside a cell so he can interrogate him. Not bleeding out in an alley somewhere. I just wanted to warn you that we don't know where Caden is. Watch your back."

Kieran grabbed the phone. "Will do." He disconnected the call.

"Hey!" she protested.

"No," he said quietly. "We have to find some kind of balance in our lives. Take advantage when we get the opportunity to be together. You've given your entire life to the Organization. I owe them and Caspar for saving me. That doesn't mean we let the Organization run our lives."

"You're right," Dakota murmured.

"I say we go up to our suite and finish what we started. Unless you've changed your mind or aren't in the mood anymore." Kieran ran his hand up her inner thigh.

"Oh," she breathed out. "Yeah, still in the mood. Of course I am."

Kieran leaned over so he could nibble her neck. With the hand he had on her body, he wiggled his fingers until he brushed over the crotch of her pants.

She arched up, trying to get more pressure, but he lifted his hand away.

"Let's go upstairs so we can lie in bed," he offered.

"With lots of pillows and blankets. Our own little fort," she said. "And —" She took the phone. "No calls." After turning her cell off, she placed the small device in the glove box.

"I love you," he told her. Kieran bent and kissed her with all the passion he'd previously held back.

Dakota was practically crawling over the middle console to get onto his lap.

"Inside," he growled.

She flung herself back with a laugh. "You make me forget where we are, what we're doing."

That was a great compliment. "Come on."

Kieran opened the SUV door and slipped out before peering around the garage. All they had to do was cross the parking lot since Dakota's assigned spot was on the first level closest to the entrance.

Dakota beeped the alarm from the key fob and Kieran winced. His senses were on high alert and that had been loud.

"Sorry," she said, meeting him at the back of the vehicle.

"It's fine." He grabbed her hand, towing her toward the hotel. Kieran kept his eyes peeled for Caden, but he wasn't picking up anything to worry about.

"It's fine," Dakota murmured. "His scent isn't here."

Kieran relaxed. He'd more than expected Caden to be waiting on them as they arrived.

Pulling open the door, Kieran ushered her inside.

She grinned then ran her finger down his chest as she brushed past him. Kieran's laugh was cut off when she froze inches inside the door.

Dread filled him. Kieran moved to press up against her back. That was when he spotted Caden blocking the elevator bank.

"Caden," Kieran greeted. "What's up, man?"

"Nothing." Caden shrugged. "I can't get hold of James or Caspar. I knew they'd been working here, so I thought I'd stop by. My access has been removed."

Dakota stepped forward and Kieran wanted to yank her back into safety. Instead he forced himself to relax his posture as Dakota walked closer to Caden.

"Yeah," Dakota said, waving her hand. "The suite's been cleaned up since the investigation is over. Jackson already has the suite rented for the weekend."

"Oh, sure." Caden smiled. "I guess that makes sense."

"Come on up," Dakota invited. She'd want to get Caden away from humans and innocents, but Kieran didn't care to have him in their home. He hadn't suspected Caden. Not once. Out of all the agents Kieran had doubted, including James, Caden hadn't pinged his radar. "We'll have a drink and celebrate the end of the case."

"I don't want to intrude," Caden replied, backing off.

"Nah, man," Kieran said. "It's been a stressful couple of days." He clamped his hand down on Caden's shoulder in a friendly gesture.

"Uh…"

Dakota swiped her card in the elevator and pressed the Call button. Kieran was glad Jackson had increased the security at the private elevators, but this was taking too long. Caden was getting nervous.

"You know, I think I'll head home," Caden told him. "You're right. It's been—"

The elevator doors opened. Dakota stuck her hand out, holding the doors open.

"You're not going anywhere," Kieran growled.

Caden's eyes widened then he smiled. "Figured it out finally?"

Kieran leaned over him. "Yeah, we did."

Caden laughed. "It took you long enough. Your father and I had a great time watching you run around. I don't see how you came from that man. He's so smart."

"Well, I do have one thing in common with my dad," Kieran agreed. He picked Caden up and tossed him into the elevator. Caden's head slammed against the metal wall before he slumped down.

Kieran stomped over to stand above the dazed agent. "Our temper."

Dakota laid her hand on his back. "We need to call this in."

Although he knew she was right, that was not how he wanted to handle the agent who'd betrayed them. This fucking shifter had put Dakota and the rest of his friends in danger.

"Give me your phone," Dakota ordered.

He glanced over his shoulder at her.

"I locked mine in the SUV, remember?"

Kieran grunted. This was going to put a damper on their plans. He pulled his cell from his pocket then tossed it to her.

As she found Remy's name, Kieran grabbed Caden by his shirt and lifted him up. "You messed up my plans for the night. I should rip out your throat."

The scent of fear filled the elevator and that made him feel better, even if his cock ached from being ignored.

Chapter Ten

Dakota rolled over before stretching her legs. It felt good to wake naturally and not have to worry about doing anything but lie back and relax. The spot beside her in bed was empty, though, and she frowned.

They'd been so exhausted after Caspar and Remy had left their suite with a subdued Caden that she and Kieran had barely managed to undress before they'd fallen in bed. Now that she'd slept, Dakota wanted nothing more than to make up for the time lost the previous night. But first she needed to find her wayward mate. She sat up in bed and opened her jaguar senses to the suite.

Fresh coffee, some type of pastry and, yes, Kieran's wonderful aroma filled the air. She sat up in bed as Kieran walked in, holding a tray from room service.

"What's this?" she asked. Dakota didn't think she'd ever seen such an amazing sight. Kieran, dressed in low-riding plaid flannel pajama bottoms, carrying the tray, with a slight blush on his face.

"I thought I'd treat you this morning," he said.

She fixed the pillows behind her back then straightened out the blankets. The suite was cool so she didn't mind the extra covers on the bed. "This is nice," she told him as Kieran set the tray over her lap. "Join me?"

"Like you even have to ask." Kieran kissed her gently before he strolled around the end of the bed to his side.

Dakota picked up her coffee and breathed deeply. *Heaven.* She glanced at Kieran, frowning. "Nu-uh."

Kieran stopped from where he was pulling back the covers. "Did you need something else?"

"Take off your pants," she demanded.

He smirked. "These?" he teased, tugging at the hem of his bottoms.

"Yes." The growl in her voice was more pronounced.

"If that's what you want." He slipped the loose pants down his legs.

She sat admiring his exquisite body until he was beside her, pulling the blankets over his lap. She stuck out her bottom lip as he covered up.

"Eat," he told her. "You're going to need your energy."

Dakota wasn't going to pass up that request. Ignoring the sight of her lover, Dakota picked up a fluffy croissant and took a big bite. She'd fuel her body then fulfill her destiny with the man she loved. Nothing was going to stop her from placing her claim on Kieran.

* * * *

Kieran stroked his cock as he waited for Dakota to finish freshening up in the bathroom. After having surprised her with breakfast in bed, he was ready to have her climb on top of him and place her claim. Instead, she'd insisted on brushing her teeth and showering.

The longer she was away, the more nervous he grew.

He'd already spoken to Caspar, Remy and Jackson earlier that morning to ensure no calls would come in. He'd even had the front desk put the *do not disturb* on the suite's phone. With his cell turned off and in the other room, Kieran had been ready.

The water shut off in the bathroom and he closed his eyes.

He wouldn't be responsible for his actions if anything interrupted them this time.

Kieran spread his legs farther then placed his hands behind his head. His erection was still standing tall and ready.

The bathroom door opened and Kieran turned his head while opening his eyes. Dakota had a towel wrapped around her body as she leaned against the doorjamb.

"Is that for me?" she asked with a purr.

Kieran grinned. "Just wanted to show you how much I want you. Want this."

Dakota's smiled was soft as well as her gaze. She walked over to the side of the bed. "It's okay to be nervous."

He nodded. "I know. I'm not nervous about you claiming me. I just don't know what to expect."

"Let me show you then." She dropped the towel before leaning forward and grasping his shaft. Dakota ran her tongue over the slit of his cock and he shivered.

"Every day I'll wake up beside you," she whispered, her breath ghosting over the head of his erection. "Every day I'll be by your side and will never let you down." She stroked him from base to tip. "Every minute of every day I'll love you."

Kieran blinked rapidly to keep the tears at bay. Her words spoke to the part inside him that had always doubted he'd be enough for anyone.

She lowered her mouth, engulfing his cock, and he moaned.

He'd lived most of his time with a chill that he could never rid himself of. But in allowing Dakota to control this moment and just letting go, a warmth filled him. He thrust up as she took him deep. It was impossible not to chase the heat that came from her.

"Dakota." He murmured her name.

"Are you ready to be mine?" she asked, hovering over him.

"Please."

She climbed up and straddled his waist. Kieran was surprised as she stopped to cup his face.

"I love you, Kieran Smith."

"I love you, Dakota Reese."

"So much," she murmured. Dakota reached behind her to hold his erection while sinking down onto him.

He shook with the need to move, but he'd let her go at her own pace. "So much," he repeated.

"You'll always be mine. You'll never be alone again," she whispered.

Kieran lost it. He lifted his hips and plunged deep. He'd never be alone because Dakota was choosing him. Out of everyone in the world, the humans, shifters and Walkers, it was Kieran who'd won her heart.

Dakota cried out with pleasure while dropping her head back.

Gripping her hips, he held her still and, with a desperate need, he thrust and plowed as he was overcome with feelings. She braced her hands on his chest while moving with him.

Their coupling was fast and furious. Kieran didn't know if he could slow down or stop. All he knew was that if he came inside her, that would signal the moment he'd strike.

"More!" she encouraged. "Almost —"

He roared then snapped his hips up.

Dakota looked like a goddess as she bowed her back, her hair flowing along her shoulders, brushing her skin.

He chased the tingle in his balls. In and out, up and down, it was him that was causing Dakota to come apart.

She screamed while clamping down on his cock while she climaxed.

"Mine!" he yelled, giving one last powerful thrust.

"Mine!" She grabbed the back of his neck, tugging him forward. Her teeth had already shifted, her fangs showing.

She bit the junction between his neck and shoulder. Cum flooded from his cock into her spasming pussy. His vision darkened and something tugged at his chest.

Dakota pulled in a mouthful of his blood and Kieran groaned as his shaft continued to pulse.

Bright lights exploded behind his eyelids and he gasped. He could see Dakota's jaguar in his mind. The strong animal stood tall with her head held back as she announced their mating to the wild. Heat spread from his chest down to the tips of his toes.

For the first time in his life, he felt connected, loved and complete.

Dakota licked at his mark before she lifted her head. "Forever."

Feeling like an entirely new man, Kieran pulled her into a hug. The missing parts of his soul had been filled. He was no longer the most powerful Walker in existence. He wasn't the Walker who had survived ten years of torture and captivity. He wasn't just another Organization agent.

He was Dakota Reese's mate.

They had their friends, their makeshift family and each other.

Kieran Smith was the luckiest man in the world.

Were Chronicles: Pack Security
Crissy Smith

Excerpt

Cassandra Wilson pushed open the bedroom balcony doors and stepped out into the cool morning air. The bite of the wind was sharp, but it cooled down her heated body. The bad dreams and sense of betrayal had her feeling ill.

She was still reeling from the events of the night before. Someone had broken into her studio and destroyed…everything. Hours of hard work ripped, torn, and broken to litter the floor. It'd appeared as if a tornado had gone through to ruin every piece she'd put her heart and soul into.

Her evening had started so normal but the end… Tears pricked her eyes again. After she'd eaten dinner with her brothers, sister-in-law and nephews, they'd taken the horses for a ride. The journey through the canyon had been freeing and she'd enjoyed the time with her family. It was nights she was able to spend in nature that helped feed her muse. Cassie knew she saw things differently from other people and believed she was blessed. On the back of her horse, she felt a connection to the world around her almost like when she was shifted. Even a short ride normally had Cassie so motivated that she'd spend the entire night in her studio.

But the previous night hadn't gone as planned. The glorious sunset and warm sensations she'd had after their ride had vanished when she'd opened her studio door and seen the destruction. Her canvases had been torn and ripped, paint splattered over the floor and walls, and every brush had been broken in half.

She had a security system and cameras but had forgotten to set them that evening. Everything that had been ruined was really her fault. Alex was forever getting on to her about remembering to set her alarm, but in the middle of the Pack territory, Cassie never worried. Now her whole life had been destroyed.

It wasn't just the loss of months of work that bothered her. She felt violated. And scared.

A knock on her bedroom door interrupted her, but she ignored it. She just wanted to be alone. Was that too much to ask? She didn't want to go to her workspace and nor did she want to talk to anyone. The police, her family, her assistant, even some of the Pack had shown up the night before. While she appreciated their support and concern, they just didn't understand. Someone had been in her house. Since her studio was located in her residence, there was no place that seemed untouched. A stranger could have gone through her things before tearing apart her creations.

She didn't know what to do now, how to act or what to say.

Her first instinct had been to hide, covers over her head, and cry, but she knew that wouldn't solve anything. As much as she wanted to pretend nothing had happened, she'd gotten up and showered to start the day. Cassie had made it as far as walking to the balcony to stare out at the territory she called her own. But that was as far as she'd made it. She just couldn't force herself to go into her studio yet.

The rapping on her door grew louder and more persistent. She suspected it was her older brother. When the door opened and Alex called her name, she sighed. Her solitude was over.

"Hey," he said as he joined her on the balcony.

Cassie glanced over her shoulder. "Hi."

"You okay?" He groaned. "That's a stupid question. I'm sorry. But what can I do to make things okay?"

She turned back to look at the sun rising above the canyon. That was the question all right. What could she do? Or Alex? Or any of them. It wasn't just Cassie who was suffering. This was the home of their family. A home they'd protected for generations.

They were lucky. The Wilson ranch was one of the few privately owned properties that shared the public canyon land. The estate had belonged to their family long before the government had come in and sectioned off acreage for a national park.

The government had tried to claim their property, too, but years of legal battles had ensured that the Wilson land would stay in the family. Cassie got to rouse every morning to one of the most beautiful views in the world. Even after the night of heartbreak she'd experienced, there was nothing like standing outside and watching the earth wake up. Alex leaned against her and she soaked up the warmth coming from him. Her oldest brother might have a tendency to hold on too tight at times, but she appreciated it more than he'd ever know. Cassie wasn't like others in the Pack. She wasn't as outgoing and was most at peace inside her studio with a paintbrush in her hand. "I don't know what to do."

"I just got off the phone with the Alpha," Alex told her. "We have a meeting with him this morning about how to handle this situation."

Knowing that she couldn't avoid the issue any longer, she turned and gave her brother her full attention. He'd set two mugs onto the rail and she hadn't noticed. She smiled and relieved him of one of the cups. The scent of fresh, strong coffee drifted up and she was grateful. She was extremely dependent on caffeine to carry her through long days.

"What time?" she asked before taking a drink. Flavor burst over her tongue—she knew her sister-in-law must have made the coffee that morning. Alex tended to make his more sludge-like.

"An hour," he replied.

So soon. Which made sense, because their Alpha would want to make sure she was safe. The traits that made her Alpha such a great leader were always right on the surface. Alpha Shawn was strong, dedicated, and fierce. She couldn't have wished for a better protector.

"You're going to get tired of everyone asking you if you're okay," Alex commented. "Just remember that we do it because we love you."

To have time to phrase her answer correctly, she took another long drink. Her brother always worried. He said it was because as the eldest, so he was responsible for her and their younger brother, Jacob. Cassie just thought he was a worry wart.

"I'll be fine," she assured him.

"Cas." There was a growl in his tone.

"I just don't understand. Why would someone break in and destroy my stuff?" She shook his head. "Why? Alex, I've never done anything to anyone."

"Fuck." Alex kissed the top of her head. "I want to tear out the throat of whoever did this."

That shouldn't make me feel good, should it? Instead of trying to get her brother to calm down, Cassie wanted to sic him on whoever had invaded her privacy. But she had to be an adult. "Is it because…we're shifters?"

"Hopefully, we'll find out. Alpha Shawn is concerned about the publicity you've gotten lately. That's one of the reasons he wants to meet."

Publicity? She snorted. Most artists wanted to receive credit for their work. All Cassie had ever needed was to paint. Her parents had supported her through the beginning stages and after their death, Alex had continued with encouragement. She'd made a good living, then the shifters had announced their presence and became public. There had been a surprising demand for her work after that.

The strangest part to her was that the Pack hadn't gone public with the others. Alpha Shawn had decided to remain in secret. The fact that her art was considered as an authentic representation of the shifter world by both humans and shifters was surprising.

And a little uncomfortable.

The press constantly pressured her about her knowledge of shifters. She'd gotten to the point where she didn't do interviews anymore. She just wanted to paint. She didn't really care about the rest of it.

"I never meant to draw attention to us."

Alex hugged her. "Ah, honey, there's nothing to be done about it. I'm proud of you. So is our Alpha. We'll get to the bottom of this and it'll all work out. I promise."

She wanted to believe him, but the wound was too fresh. She hoped Alpha Shawn had some ideas. He was one of the smartest men she knew and just a tad devious.

"I spoke to James also," Alex said. "He's going to bring over everything we have in storage and order more supplies for you. We'll have you back to work before you know it."

Cassie always had back-up supplies. She lived in the guesthouse and her studio was one of the rooms. At the main house, where Alex lived, he kept a supply room for her so she didn't have to have an order rushed to her.

"I'm almost ready for the show anyway." She was supposed to be having a showing in less than a month. "If we even still have it."

"We'll have it," Alex said. "I told you not to worry about it."

She nodded and stopped herself from telling him she was going to worry anyway. The threat they'd received in the mail to stop the show or else still weighed on her mind. Even though everyone told her it wasn't her fault, she knew it was. The crazy Church that had been after the shifters for months now had narrowed in on her town.

"We'll talk about it with Alpha Shawn. He is aware of the threat and has Chase looking into it."

"Okay," she relented. It was never worth arguing with Alex. He would eventually get his way by wearing her down. Hopefully Shawn could talk some sense into him. He was one of the few people Alex listened to.

"Let's go then." Her brother motioned her back inside.

Cassie followed him through her bedroom and into the hallway. Her house consisted of four bedrooms, a living room, a kitchen and a small fenced-in area for a backyard. The guesthouse was just yards away from the main residence where Alex lived.

Alex hadn't even wanted her this far, though. He'd tried to talk her into just remodeling a portion of the main residence, but Cassie needed space. She was an adult and way past living under the same roof as her brother. Plus, she'd gotten to design the entire place. She loved every inch of her home. And she was close enough to her brothers, sister-in-law and nephews to see them every day.

Jacob and Peyton resided a couple of miles down the hill in their own home. They had a nice six-bedroom dwelling that fit their family perfectly. Jacob worked for the Parks and Wildlife Department stationed in the canyon. Peyton stayed home and took care of their boys, one aged four and one aged six. Cassie enjoyed having her family so close to her most of the time. However, she would've preferred a little more distance right then. Alex strolled through her place like he belonged there. She didn't comment as she followed him. Normally Alex tried to show her that he respected her space, although once in a while, he went overprotective on her.

Since she'd found the destruction the night before, Alex had been in full alpha male mode. She would never admit it to him, but his protectiveness was easing some of her fear.

The drive to the Alpha compound took thirty minutes. Shawn lived deeper in the canyon. If they'd taken the horses, it would have only been ten minutes.

Not all members of the pack lived inside the canyon. Most had houses and businesses in town. Only the oldest families had claim to any canyon land.

As he drove, Alex talked about the horses and his upcoming plans for the ranch. Cassie had heard it all before, so she was able to tune him out and respond with some sounds.

By the time they arrived at the large Alpha cabin, she'd almost fallen asleep. She'd barely slept at all the previous night and was bone-tired. The winding roads that led to the house, and the familiar trip, soothed her further.

Her brother stopped the truck and patted her knee. "Let's get this over with, then you can get some real sleep. I can tell you didn't get a wink."

"Yeah, okay," she agreed and pushed her door open.

There were other vehicles parked nearby, but that wasn't a surprise. She'd never been to Alpha Shawn's when the house didn't have several guests. Having all those Pack members around would drive her crazy. She couldn't stand to have people constantly underfoot. It was one of the other reasons she lived in the guesthouse instead of the main home. Alex worked from home, and Cassie couldn't handle all the people who came in and out to do business with him.

The door opened before they reached it and her Alpha stepped out. Shawn Mathewson stood on the porch and opened his arms. He was an attractive man with dark skin and hair, his eyes and smile dazzling her. The power that rolled off him could be quite intimidating, but he was truly a good man and a great leader.

She grinned and walked up the stairs where her Alpha engulfed her. He held her tightly then patted her shoulder.

Taking a step back, she peered up at the impressive man in front of her. Just being in his presence helped calm the wolf inside her, which had been agitated since she'd found the break-in.

"Let's go inside," he said, placing his arm around her shoulder.

They entered his home and went through to the living room. Cassie saw the Beta of the pack, Chase Lawson. She inclined her head toward him in respect.

"Hey, sweetie," he greeted. "You doing okay?"

Cassie nodded. "As well as can be expected."

"We'll find out who did this."

A promise that she knew Chase would do his best to keep. The Lawson family had been part of the Pack for as long as hers had. Chase owned the local diner and was one of the best cooks in the area. She made a point of stopping by for home-cooked meals as often as possible.

He always greeted her with a smile and a kind word. He was Alex's age and the two had grown up together as the best of friends since they'd started school.

Chase welcomed Alex with a hug and a manly slap on the back while Alpha Shawn moved Cassie to the couch, taking a seat with her. Alex sat across from her in one of the chairs and, after making four mugs of coffee, Chase passed them around before he joined them.

Cassie placed both hands on the large cup as she settled back in the corner of the couch. She felt protected and secure with the three men. If she closed her eyes, she had no doubt she would be fine.

Their voices flowed over her as they discussed who could have been responsible and why. Cassie couldn't imagine anyone who would have wanted to destroy her work. Even with the shifter controversy, she was only an artist.

"We're just guessing here." Alpha Shawn's words drew her out of her thoughts. "And until we get to the bottom of this, the entire Pack will be on high alert. I don't want anyone alone. I'll double the guards around town and here."

"Cassie can stay at the main house," Alex added.

"Wait!" She sat up straight. "I'm not moving out of my house."

Three sets of eyes turned to her.

"No." She shook her head. "I have to work hard to make up for the canvases that I lost."

"It's just temporary," Alex assured her.

"I'll set the alarm. I'm sorry I forget. And we have the cameras."

"Cass." Alex leaned forward and braced his forearms on his knees. "It's more than that. We don't know who or why someone did this. Luckily, you weren't home but…"

Cassie saw the struggle on his face. He was concerned about her.

She set her mug down and spoke directly to him. "But if I just move to the main house, then they win."

"This isn't about winning! This is about keeping you safe!"

Cassie ignored the rise of Alex's voice. "I'm not giving up my house."

"Yes, you are!"

"Hold on!" Alpha Shawn tried to interrupt.

"No, I'm not. I'm a big girl and I can take care of myself."

Alex rose and towered over her. "You…are…staying in the main house." Each word was clipped.

She seldom argued with him, but she just couldn't give in this time. She'd worked hard to gain her independence after their parents' death. She was thirty years old and refused to be treated like she was five.

"No."

Alex stepped forward, but Chase stood and got between them. "How about a compromise?"

Both she and Alex turned to him.

Chase motioned Alex back down and waited until he had settled again before taking his own seat.

"What's your idea?" Alpha Shawn asked.

"Well, you know Max is back. He's working in the diner right now, but we can use him as Cassie's personal security."

Max Lawson, Cassie mused. She hadn't seen Chase's elder brother in a long time. He was older than both Alex and Chase so Cassie hadn't been around him much growing up. By the time Max had left the Pack at seventeen to join the Navy, she'd only been seven. She knew about him because he was the Pack's only non-shifter. Not that he was human. Max was a shifter. He carried the DNA that made them different from humans. However, Max was unable to shift into his animal. Cassie didn't know much about non-shifters, but Alpha Shawn had never allowed Max to be treated any differently, from what she could remember.

There were rumors about Max being part of one of the elite Navy Seal teams in the military, but that could have been all talk.

Alpha Shawn was smiling. "I like that idea."

Cassie wasn't so sure. "I don't really think I need personal security. I hardly even leave the property." She just didn't feel right about having someone follow her around all the time. Yes, the situation was scary, but assigning a bodyguard? It was a little too much.

"I disagree," her Alpha said. "The break-in was at your residence. Max would be able to keep an eye on you and look into who might have been responsible."

She knew the expression on his face. Alpha Shawn had made up his mind.

"I'll spend most of my time in the studio anyway," she argued. "He'll be in my way."

Chase chuckled. "I promise he won't."

Knowing she was coming up against a wall, she sighed. "This is stupid."

Alpha Shawn reached over and patted her knee. "Then just humor me. I want you safe."

"Fine." She rolled her eyes. She would make the best of the situation—she always did. Besides, how bad could it be? Chase was a good guy, so she doubted that Max was much different.

* * * *

Max Lawson pulled the skillets off the stove then dropped them into the sink full of soapy water. He stretched his arms over his head and rolled his neck. He liked working at the Canyon Café with his brother, even if it was dissimilar from what he had always done before. The most important thing was that he had something to do. He could concentrate on a task and not have to think or remember.

Not having enough to do worried him and made him nervous, so he was glad for the hard work.

"Hey, Max!"

He glanced over his shoulder and saw his brother in the doorway. "Hey, bro."

His brother had been summoned to the Alpha house earlier that morning, leaving Max to handle the breakfast rush for him.

"Got a minute?" Chase tilted his head, indicating that Max should join him out front.

"Sure." Max turned and followed him out of the kitchen into the dining area.

The rush was over. Only a few customers were still eating. Sue Ellen was taking care of the patrons, so Max didn't have to worry about them. He always liked being in the back more than waiting tables.

He'd only been home about six months, so when the Pack members saw him, they wanted to know about his time away. And Max honestly couldn't talk about it. Too much of what he'd done was still classified.

Chase took a seat on one of the chairs in front of the counter, next to another man. Max followed but remained back where the scarred countertop separated them. He still didn't like to be too close to people.

Once he reached the two, he recognized Alex Wilson. Chase and Alex had remained tight, even as the years passed and they'd found different interests. Max grinned at Alex and offered his hand. "Nice to see you again, Alex."

They shook hands and Alex smiled. Max tucked his hands behind his back. Just the small, polite gesture of shaking was hard. He didn't want Chase to see his struggles, though. Being Beta of the pack was hard enough. At least he got to share the role with Alex, the two of them having someone by their sides. It reminded Max of how he'd been with the men in his unit. The men he'd promised to protect.

"You too. Glad you made it back safe."

Max nodded but didn't say anything. Yes, he had returned safely, but… No, he couldn't think about that now. Instead, he noticed his brother's obvious worry. Max offered Chase a small smile before giving his full attention to Alex.

The Wilson family was one of the oldest members of the Pack. Chase, of course, was closer to them, living as a Pack, but Max still had a connection with the family. He'd been out of the country when he'd received word that the Wilson parents had been killed in an accident.

Chase had been devastated and had told him how hard it had been on the kids. It seemed Alex had stepped up and done a good job getting his siblings through the grieving process.

"Coffee?" Max picked up the pot from under the counter.

Chase and Alex nodded.

He poured three cups then slid the first two across to them. "So, what's going on?"

They exchanged a look that stood the hair up on the back of Max's neck. "What?"

"We need your help," Alex said.

"Of course," he offered. He would do whatever he could to help any of the Pack members. Even though he hadn't quite fit in with the kids growing up, they had never been mean to him. Their Alpha would not have allowed it.

Max didn't understand why he was different from everyone else. What had gone wrong to make him unable to shift? But it was what it was and there was nothing he could do about it.

"Good." Chase drew his attention. "Do you remember Cassandra?"

"Your younger sister?" he asked Alex. He could picture the freckle-face girl with skinned knees, running around in shorts. She had always been tagging behind Alex and Chase as the boys had grown up. "Sort of."

Alex nodded. "We need security for her."

"Why?"

As Alex and Chase filled him in on what was going on, Max found himself growing angry. He knew he had to get a handle on his reaction, though. After his last mission, he had gone through a debriefing and had been shown several techniques to control himself. The military did not want him to go off on civilians.

But the thought of anyone threatening a member of his Pack made his blood boil. He listened intently as Alex explained the entire situation.

"What do you need from me?" he asked when the man was finished.

"Cassie won't agree to move into the main house. She wants to stay in her residence and studio. I'm not comfortable with her being alone."

"You want me to watch over her?" he asked, surprised. He wasn't a guard. He didn't have a position with the Pack. His brother was the Alpha's second, his Beta, but after Max had left for the Navy, he'd given up any rank within the Pack.

"Yes," Chase answered. "Alpha Shawn agreed. We're doubling all security for the Pack, but we want Cassie to have someone with her full-time."

Max owed his Alpha a lot for always supporting him. Hell, he owed his brother, too. Chase had welcomed him back with open arms. His brother let Max stay in his house and had given him a job. "Okay, when do you want me to start?"

Alex sighed heavily and dropped his head. "Thank you."

Max wasn't a touchy-feely kind of guy. Normally he did everything he could to avoid contact with others, but he found himself reaching over and patting Alex's shoulder. "Sure, I'm glad to help."

"I knew you would be," Chase said proudly.

Max warmed to his brother's praise.

"Chase can go over everything with you." Alex stood. "I need to get back to the house. Cassie is with Jacob right now, but he has to work today."

Max nodded and waited until Alex was out of the door before turning to his brother. "What else?"

Chase rubbed his hands roughly over his face. "Alpha Shawn is concerned about the publicity the gallery is getting. Several of the artists, Cassie in particular, have gotten a lot of attention. Last week we received a threat that if we didn't cancel the upcoming show, we would regret it. It was from the Church for Humanity, the people the wolves have had problems with ever since we went public. Our Pack didn't go public, and Shawn isn't sure how much longer he can hide us if the Church has targeted us."

"Is that really a big concern? From what I've seen, there have only been a few issues since the shifters announced their presence."

"It's a concern," Chase told him. "The Coalition between all the shifter species is brand-new. We're hoping that will protect all shifters, but until we know for sure, we still want to remain secret. Some of the human lawmakers are talking about forcing shifters to register."

"Register?"

"Yeah, so they can have a database on all of us."

"That's not right," Max said in disgust.

"I know. Shawn is talking with the council about what we can do, but he's worried."

"Well, I'll do what I can," Max promised.

"Good. How are you feeling?"

He knew his brother was concerned. Chase might not know everything that had gone down with his last mission, but his brother knew him well. Chase had also witnessed some of his nightmares.

"I'm fine."

Chase didn't look like he believed him but didn't push. "Scott's coming in. I thought we could grab your stuff, then I'll follow you over to the Wilson ranch."

"Sure." Max picked up the empty coffee cups. "Let me just finish cleaning up real quick."

"Okay, I have to grab a few things from the office, anyway."

Max went back into the kitchen to wash the last of the pans he'd used earlier. He didn't like leaving a mess. His brother might own the diner, but Max always pulled his weight. He hoped he would be an asset for the Wilson family. He remembered they had always been so happy. Very similar to his own. They'd never treated him any different either.

He was scrubbing the last pan when Scott Little walked in the back door.

"Hey, man!" Scott waved at him.

Max inclined his head since his hands were still in the water. "Thanks for coming."

"No problem," Scott assured him. "Didn't have anything planned today anyway."

Scott attended the community college in the next town over and was an okay kid. Max enjoyed their shifts together as well as Scott's quirky humor.

"You about ready?" Chase called from the front of the diner.

Max rinsed off the pan then placed it in the strainer. "Yeah."

He waved to Scott as he joined his brother out front. He grabbed his jacket and keys from under the counter. Together, they left.

One of his first purchases when he'd returned to the States had been his Harley. Chase had tried to get him to use one of the Alpha's many vehicles, but Max enjoyed riding the bike. He craved the freedom that the motorcycle provided him.

He'd found that the best time to ride down the canyon was just before sunset. The gorgeous views on the back of his Harley could not be seen the same way in a truck or an SUV. Max threw his leg over the bike and turned the key. The machine came alive under him. He couldn't suppress his grin. Yes, motorcycles were dangerous, and he loved every single second he was on his.

Chase waved at him as he climbed inside his truck.

Chase's house was just outside the city limits. He needed to be close to the Alpha in case any problems arose. The fifteen-minute ride was smooth and without a lot of traffic. Max's brother was ahead of him as they both drove in the same direction.

The Wilson ranch was farther inside the canyon lands. He would be able to take his bike there and hopefully would have time to ride some of the private roads. Plus, there was good hiking around the Wilson place. He didn't know if Cassie Wilson hiked, but he sure hoped so. It would be nice to be able to get some fresh air and just be away from everyone and everything.

He pulled up beside his brother's truck then turned the engine off. Chase's abode was small compared to a lot of the other Pack houses. But the three-bedroom structure was enough for them. Chase had welcomed the company when Max had come back to town. Their parents had offered to let Max stay with them. However, he was glad Chase had suggested they live together. He loved his mom and dad, but at forty, he didn't want to live with them again.

"I'm going to take a shower while you get your things together," Chase informed him.

Max nodded and made his way to his bedroom. He didn't have a lot. Just clothes and a few things he'd kept in storage. Even the furniture in the bedroom was his brother's.

Finally, Max felt like he was putting roots down. Eventually, he would buy his own home and concentrate on discovering what he wanted to do with the rest of his life. Whether he'd stay in Canyon or move on, he wasn't sure. He had time to decide.

He grabbed two duffels out of his closet then started to pack. He didn't know how long he would be needed at the Wilson ranch. It was better to have too much stuff than to have to leave Cassandra to go pick up what he needed.

He threw in jeans, T-shirts, boxers, socks and a light jacket. Back at his closet, he reached up to the top shelf and brought down the lock box. Max carried the box to the bed and sat.

It had been six months since he'd opened it.

He removed the keys from his pocket and carefully unlocked then lifted the lid. Inside was his favorite gun. A .45 Desert Eagle.

He ran his fingers over the stainless-steel barrel and sighed. He hadn't held a weapon in his hand since he'd left the Navy. He wasn't sure he would even be able to fire it again.

As he sat on the bed, he could still smell the smoke from the last gunfight. He hadn't been shooting his Desert Eagle that day. The M4 that he'd had on his shoulder had run out of ammo and Max had looked down in horror when he'd realized the entire team had used all the bullets they'd brought with them.

The house they'd been hiding in was small. Evan Cruise had lain at Max's feet, wounded and crying out in pain.

Deep down, he'd feared that was it. They were all going to die over in some godawful place and no one would know all they had wanted to do was rescue the captured aid workers.

The missions were classified and Max wondered if Evan's family would even be given his body.

The guerilla fighters who had gotten the jump on them had still been shooting into the house. Max had knelt beside his friend and gripped Evan's hand. He'd been in charge of his five-man team. It'd been up to him to get them out.

"You okay?"

Max started at Chase's voice. He slammed the lid closed on the gun box and stood. Quickly, he stuffed the container at the top of one of the duffels and faced his brother. "Yeah, just about done."

Concern was evident on Chase's face. Max had to ignore it. He wasn't ready to talk about what he'd been through. Actually, he couldn't speak to anyone about anything. He rushed into the bathroom then quickly packed everything he would need for the next several days.

When he returned to the bedroom, Chase was zipping up one of the bags. Max dumped his toiletries into the other then closed it. They each grabbed one as they headed out of the door. Max was relieved that Chase wasn't pushing him. He knew that he would have to share something with Chase soon. At the moment, his brother was giving him time.

"I'll take your bags over for you," Chase offered.

"Thanks." He passed the second duffel to his brother. Ready to go, he strode to the bike.

He could probably find the Wilson ranch on his own, but any time he had a flashback he was always a little shaky. He needed a few minutes to get his bearings, but he would have to follow Chase so he wouldn't get lost.

Chase backed out and Max waited until the dust settled, then followed. He was happy to have something to keep his thoughts off what he'd been through.

Hopefully this new job would help him clear his mind.

It took longer than he expected to reach the Wilson property. He slowed at the large gate where Chase was waiting. His brother waved him through and Max drove on. He pulled off to the side as Chase closed and locked the gate again.

Max was glad to see that they were indeed taking precautions on security.

Chase climbed back into his truck and started south. Max followed, using his senses to get familiar with the area. The main house loomed in the distance, a strong, solid structure that appeared inviting. Max could remember the barbecues that he and his family attended there when he was younger.

Even with the passing of their parents, it looked like the Wilson children had kept the property up. Green grass filled both sides of the paved road. As he pulled next to his brother and turned off his motorcycle, he could hear horses not far from him.

He turned his head to see if he could spot them and couldn't. He hadn't ridden in over a decade. His family didn't keep animals, and in the service, he hadn't had the opportunity. Excitement had him swinging off his bike. He'd always enjoyed the freedom of being on the back of one of the large animals. Luckily, even though the horses could sense the predator in a shifter, as long as a mount was treated with respect it didn't have any problems accepting shifters as riders or caregivers. The stallions and mares sure were trusting. In that regard, Max was envious of them.

"They still have horses?"

Chase nodded. "Yeah, Alex puts a lot of time into them."

"I thought he worked in the gallery."

Chase waved his hand. "He does. But his love will always be the horses first."

The front door opened and the subject of their conversation stepped out. "Hey, guys."

Smiling widely, Alex stomped down the stairs to greet them. He'd changed out of his slacks into jeans. Max was relieved to see Alex more relaxed, and glad he had agreed to help. It was great to be needed again.

They shook hands and Alex motioned toward the house. "Cassie's inside. Let's talk here before you go over to the house."

Max nodded and followed Alex and his brother.

The cool air hit him as soon as he walked inside. Max hadn't noticed just how hot he was until the air conditioning blew over him.

He must have made a sound, because Alex glanced back at him. "Cassie keeps the air on frigid. She can't stand being hot."

Since Max had spent way too much time in deserts and jungles, he agreed with her. "Feels good."

Alex grinned. "You'll fit in just fine."

He hung back, taking in the homey feel of the ranch house. The Wilsons had money, but he wasn't uncomfortable walking through the hall. The simple touches around the place were welcoming, not intimidating.

The hall opened into a large living room with beautiful wood flooring. Dark-brown leather couches dominated the space and a huge flat-screen television was placed over the stone hearth. In the corner, standing by the curved bar, was the most gorgeous woman he'd ever seen.

She smiled wide when their gazes met. "Wow! You grew up."

Max opened his mouth to respond then closed it again quickly. There was no way this sexy creature in front of him was Cassie Wilson. Gone were the braids and the crooked teeth. Instead, she had a pixie cut of short brown hair with streaks of blonde. She had to be only five foot five or so. She was tanned and had a body built for a man's hands. He had to clench his teeth to keep from reaching out for her.

He groaned mentally. Not what he had expected. Cassie Wilson was an attractive woman. Her soft chocolate eyes sparkled with amusement as she licked her lips.

Fuck! His cock hardened painfully. Max struggled to push aside his carnal needs and remember there were two other people in the room.

Home of Erotic Romance

Sign up for our newsletter and find out about all our romance book releases, eBook sales and promotions, sneak peeks and FREE romance eBooks!

About the Author

Crissy Smith lives in Texas with her husband, daughter, and three Labrador retrievers. The three dogs love to curl up under her computer desk and nap while she writes. It doesn't leave a lot of room for her but what's a woman to do?

When not writing or reading, she enjoys hunting, camping and shooting. But she has a girly side too and is addicted to pedicures and coffee.

She has been writing since she was a teenager and still loves everything to do with the paranormal. Her stories and characters all have a place in her heart. She loves the Alpha male, the dominant werewolf, and the Master vampire, which find their way in most of her books.

Learn more about the characters she has created at her website where they have their very own page. It will be updated from time to time to let you know what's going on with them. Also you can find out who will be in the next book.

Crissy loves to hear from readers. You can find her contact information, website details and author profile page at https://www.totallybound.com